DINNER AT THE *Deli*

MARSHA CASPER COOK

ISBN: 978-1-970730-93-7

For more about Marsha please visit

www.MarshaCasperCook.com
www.MarshasKidsBooks.com
www.MichiganAvenueMedia.com

Published by

Fideli Publishing, Inc.
119 W. Morgan St.
Martinsville, IN 46151

www.FideliPublishing.com

Sometimes a dream is just a dream.
And a wish is just a thought.

"Love is passion, obsession, someone you can't live without. I say, fall head over heels. Find someone you can love like crazy and who will love you the same way back. How do you find him? Well, you forget your head and you listen to your heart. And I'm not hearing any heart. Cause the truth is, honey, there's no sense living your life without this. To make the journey and not fall deeply in love, well, you haven't lived a life at all. But you have to try, 'cause if you haven't tried, you haven't lived."

— William Parrish in Meet Joe Black

Who will be remembered as time passes?

Will it be for something small but unique,

Or will it be for something powerful and splendid?

Will it be a smile,

Or a tear,

Or loving someone very dear?

Will it be for a friendship that flows like fine wine,

Or will it be for living with joy and commitment,

Happiness and good fortune?

Will it be for the legacy of love

That will shine forever,

Or for the memories shared,

Or that special feeling when you think of them,

And the ones you will never let go,
And the fact that you have passed them to others,
so they, too, will remember?

That will be your legacy as well as theirs.

— Marsha Casper Cook 2025

A Word from Gracie

What you are about to read is true. Well, maybe not all of it. You decide. You might have a dog or a cat, and you might talk to them. Of course, you don't expect them to talk back to you—but think about it for just a minute. They look at you and understand your emotions. When you're sad, so are they. And when you're happy, they know it.

I'm a dog. I'm also an angel who, for whatever reason, seems to have good luck finding the good in relationships. Everyone has a guardian angel. Usually, they send me to people who need me, but there are times when I don't get it right. I'm always hopeful I can do whatever needs to be done, but sometimes I need help.

Hello Deli

Hello Deli was more than a successful restaurant; it was a place where people could go, enjoy a meal, and see the same faces year after year. It was like a family, not just a spot for great corned beef and chicken noodle soup.

Zach Feldman owned and operated this joyful place. But as the years went by, he grew worried about what would happen when he died. Zach didn't want to be morbid, but he knew he wasn't going to live forever. He didn't love thinking about it, but it was the truth.

Zach's grandson, Adam, could have ended those worries, but he lived in New York and wasn't about to leave his fancy high-paying job to come back to Chicago. Adam wouldn't be the one to continue his legacy, and Zach loved him too much to ever to be mad, but the reality was he had no one to take over the deli.

When Adam was very young, he would help Zach every Saturday and Sunday. The customers loved him, and all the servers and kitchen staff considered him family. Instead of taking a job there, he went to college and graduate school. After a quick trip to New York City, he decided that was where he wanted to live the rest of his life. He became successful there, and that was that. No matter how hard Zach tried, there was no way Adam would move back to run the business.

Zach had accepted that things probably weren't going to change, but sometimes change comes into a life without the slightest warning.

Joe, one of Zach's oldest and favorite customers, came to him with a request. Joe was moving to a glamorous condo downtown that didn't allow dogs. He knew Zach had often talked about getting a dog but never did, so Joe asked if he'd be willing to take Gracie.

Zach was not one to look a gift horse in the mouth. He opened his door and his heart to Gracie, the cutest Cavalier King Charles spaniel he'd ever seen, and his life immediately became brighter. He didn't realize he'd been lonely until she entered his life.

At first, he had no idea how special Gracie was. But as the weeks passed, he realized she was there for a reason. Because Gracie talked—and she told him she was there to help find Adam a wife. Zach had never been a believer in the mystic world, but always believed things happened for a reason.

Living with a talking dog was challenging at first, but he eventually understood Gracie's intentions. He wanted his grandson to be happy, and Gracie had a plan for that. She shared it with him a week or so before Thanksgiving.

Chapter One

Adam Feldman was sitting at his desk, looking out at the city and pretending to listen to the phone conversation he was having. He usually had too much on his mind to pay attention to detail. Now and then, he would chime in, "Yes, I agree." Then he'd glance at his expensive watch, his latest present to himself. He was already thinking about how to spend the money he was making from this new deal.

He used to worry about money, but not anymore. It was good to be rich.

Adam was only in his mid-thirties, but sometimes he felt old after a life lived in the fast lane. He thought about his good fortune a lot but always had a fear that someone was going to take it from him. When he was younger, he got himself in a mess or two but didn't tell his grandfather or ask

Zach to bail him out. Adam was a good guy, but he could be tough when he needed to be.

He was good-looking, and getting a new woman whenever he wanted was easy. He usually wore tailored navy suits and white shirts. He liked white shirts because even if he changed clothes, they looked great with his classic jeans and expensive loafers. He had dark, curly hair that wasn't the easiest to maintain, but it looked great on him.

Adam hoped to have a wife and family someday, but he didn't always pick the best women. His girlfriends were always glamorous, but his relationships usually ended in a warm goodbye and no hard feelings. He knew that was a little shallow. But when one woman was gone, another was waiting in the wings.

He needed companionship because he didn't like to go to restaurants or business functions alone. When he first came to New York from Chicago, he dated two or three women a week. But then that got old, and he amused himself with socialites from the country club where he played golf. And when that stopped interesting him, he picked the best of the bunch, a gorgeous blonde with green eyes.

Her name was Gabriella. She had a great sense of style and left a lasting impression when she walked into a room. Adam liked that, even if they didn't communicate well.

Gabriella wasn't much for conversation, especially when she was watching her soaps. She never asked him questions or checked in about his day; it was all about her. But she looked good, and Adam couldn't help but admit that was important to him.

She wasn't really marriage material, but Adam figured as long as they didn't actually walk down the aisle, it would be easy enough to cut ties whenever he decided that was necessary. It wasn't an ideal relationship, but it worked for now.

* * *

So, there Adam was, still looking out the window, reminding himself that money hadn't made him as happy as he thought it would. But that was how it was.

He grabbed his coat and headed to meet his ride. Adam hadn't driven himself to work for a long time, and driving in New York was far worse than even the insane Chicago traffic.

"Damn," he called out; it was cold as the wind hit him smack in the face. His driver, Lewis, was smoking a cigar next to the car.

"Tough day, Adam?"

"Just like the others." Adam laughed.

"Are you going home tonight or to Miss Gabriella's?"

"Going home to a martini with lots of olives. Want to join us? I'm sure Martin has plenty. He's like my grandmother. She cooked for ten people when maybe three were eating."

"Reminds me of mine. Damn, she was a good cook."

Adam smiled. "My grandfather cooked even more than she did, but bringing home food isn't a big deal when you own a deli. So, will you join us?"

"Can't tonight."

"Hot date?"

"My daughter's got a concert. She plays the violin. She's good. Although what father's going to say his daughter isn't?"

They both laughed. Adam never thought much about having kids. He realized there were many single moms and single dads, and nobody minded anymore, but he figured he needed a wife for that. He barely got through the day himself, let alone taking care of a kid or two.

"Here we are," Lewis said as they pulled up to Adam's building. "Stay warm. See you at eight."

"Listen, you've got a lot going on tonight. Let's make it ten."

"Really?"

"Have fun tonight. I can start from home and then go in. Might be good for me."

As soon as Adam got off the elevator, he heard singing. He smiled, thinking Martin had a date. They'd been friends since they were kids, and Adam knew him well. When Martin was filled with vocal jubilation, he was usually going out for the night.

"So, you got a date?" Adam asked even before he took off his coat.

"I do. She's gorgeous. A redhead. You heard me singing?"

"As soon as I walked off the elevator. The entire building could probably hear."

Martin poured a martini for Adam and smiled. "I'm sure she has a friend. Do you want to join us? It will be fun. You need some fun in your life. Work isn't everything."

"I'm going to lie on the couch and relax. And if I didn't work as hard, we wouldn't be here chitchatting. I'd be out there struggling to make a buck."

"Looks like it's extra olives in your martini tonight."

"As many as you can fit."

"Bad day?"

"Sort of. But it could have been worse. I had a dinner to go to, but I skipped it. I used to enjoy those dinners, but they're not fun anymore."

"Luckily, it's paid off for you," Martin said. "Tomorrow will be better."

"Isn't that what you always say?"

"It is, but I knew in a minute you would say that tomorrow is a great new day. I just beat you to the punch."

"Guess we know each other pretty well." Adam slid onto the couch. "Too bad neither of us has a woman who cares to know us the way we know each other."

"Isn't that the definition of best friends? Thank goodness we have each other. I would never have had the courage to leave Chicago."

"You just needed to start over."

"Bad luck can do that to you."

"It wasn't about luck. Rachel died, and you did everything for her. Think about how lucky Rachel was to have you at her side when she needed you the most. Being a good guy's not such a bad thing."

"I guess you're right."

"I know I am. I wish I could be a little more like you."

"I never turned the corner to making money. Without you, I'd probably never be able to live in such style."

"Sure you would have. You were a great chef and a fabulous bartender. You still are. You make the best martini ever."

"I worked in a diner that didn't make money and didn't serve liquor, so what good did it do me?"

"It meant you could pay the bills and still care for Rachel."

"Without you and your grandfather, I would have been in debt for the rest of my life."

"But you're not." Adam paused. "And I'm glad you moved here."

"How in the hell did we get from martinis to this conversation?" Martin asked.

"I guess it's my fault. I've been feeling sorry for myself lately. I need to make some changes. 'Poor me' isn't my style. I have no idea how I let myself get out of whack. I need a recharge, but I don't even know where to begin."

Martin perked up. "I have a great idea."

"What is it?"

"I'll tell you a little later. I want to approach it just right."

"Come on, don't keep me in suspense."

"In time, my good man. I don't want to spoil our fun little talk. We hardly have these anymore."

"Alright. In the meantime, I have a question that's been bothering me for days."

"Fine, let it out."

"Well, here goes. I've been having a dream."

Martin looked at Adam and grinned. "You told me you never dream."

"Well, I do now," Adam confessed. He knew this would be strange, but he had to tell someone, and Martin understood him better than anyone.

"So, tell me. What kind of dreams are you having?"

"I just figured I should tell you. And since we're being open and honest about everything, there's something more important you should know. And don't go crazy when I tell you this."

"Should I have another drink?"

"Might be a good idea." Adam got up and poured each of them another martini.

Martin took his drink, sat back in the chair, crossed his leg, and was ready for whatever Adam had to say. "Okay, shoot."

"Here goes. I asked Gabriella to marry me."

Instead of sipping his martini, Martin gulped it down. "What the hell?"

"Yeah, I know. It seemed like a good idea at the time. She fits the bill."

"Have you lost your mind?"

"I think I have. And now her parents are planning this glamorous wedding."

"Well, here's to your marriage?" Martin held up his empty glass. "To the groom."

"Okay, I get the message."

"Good. You know love matters. When I think of Rachel, I remember her sweetness and the immense love I had for her. I will never find anyone like her. Love like that doesn't just happen."

"I know. She was special."

"I'll never find anyone who can take her place. If she hadn't died, I'd be with her and I would never let her go. That's what love is."

Adam nodded. "I want that kind of love, but I don't think that's in the cards. My person doesn't exist."

Martin looked his best friend straight in the eye. "Listen to me. She's out there, but Gabriella isn't the one."

"How do you know that?"

"Because I think you don't love her. I don't even think you like her."

Adam didn't respond at first. He wondered why Martin was telling him what he already knew. Adam had many girl-friends over the years, but Martin didn't say much about the others because they never lasted longer than a few months. One almost made it a year.

"Well, you're right. I don't love her. And, on many occasions, I don't like her."

"Then don't marry her."

"I didn't give it much thought. It was one of those in-the-moment things."

"Are you playing a joke on me? Okay, I get it, tell me it's not true. You know how I feel about marriage."

Martin wasn't fond of Gabriella, and the feeling was mutual. She rarely talked to him; when she did, it was only to order him around or dismiss him. She never understood that Martin and Adam were brothers by choice.

"Speaking of your beloved," Martin said, "she called five times. She left a message three times and forgot she had left a previous one."

"If you were home, why didn't you answer?"

"It was fun listening to her messages."

"Wonder why she called on the house phone."

"Probably to irritate me. You know she likes that."

"Yes, she does." Adam laughed. "I think she likes you. She just likes playing jokes on you."

"I don't think she's just kidding around. She's way too serious for that."

Adam laughed. Gabriella was beautiful, but sometimes she didn't think. Adam also knew he paid little, if any, attention to her moods. He knew he should probably do a better job and think things through. Not doing that was how he ended up getting engaged.

"I'm sorry," Adam said. "I should have told you earlier. It's just that the subject never came up."

Martin laughed. "Why would it? Do you think that I was going to ask whether you got engaged without telling anyone?"

"No, but maybe now wasn't a good time."

"What? You were going to get married secretly, move in here with her. And one day she would walk out of the bedroom, sit down to breakfast, and say, 'Martin, dear, Adam and I tied the knot. And we didn't invite you to the wedding because I know you don't like me.'"

"You know that would never happen. We're like brothers. Remember our oath—through thick and thin, in and out, we tell the truth, good or bad. It's you and me." Adam recited this while holding his hand up like in a court of law.

"Yes, I know our code."

"We'll have a prenup; you know she doesn't need my money. Her father has more money than God, so it's no big deal."

"This is your dream life?"

"No, that's just it. Remember how I said I've had dreams lately? The night I asked Gabriella to marry me, I had this dream. It was so vivid it was like it was happening in real time."

"What was the dream about?"

"There was this dog. And she was sitting on my bed, talking to me like a friend."

"Keep going. What did she tell you?"

"The dog was a King Charles spaniel like the one on the first floor. She told me to call her Gracie...Never mind, maybe I'm crazy. Let's forget it."

"No, it's okay. Go on."

"She said she could help me find love. And that the woman I'm with now isn't for me."

"Well, that's good news. There's hope."

"There's more. She said love is like a journey and she wants to help me, but I need to follow my heart when I meet the right woman. That I'll feel like she is the only one for me, and that feeling will be so strong I won't be able to ignore it. Gracie said it's going to surprise me and I shouldn't ignore the way it happens."

"Well, thank goodness she says it's not Gabriella."

"Well, there's one more thing. The dog had wings like an angel."

"That's weird, but it was just a dream."

"No, it wasn't just one time. For the last week, she's been sitting on my bed. Every time I wake up, she says hello and then she's gone. So, what do you think?"

Martin took a long breath and smiled. "Well, I guess you'll just have to wait and see."

"Is that all you have to say?"

"Pretty much. If she really is an angel, you can't fight heaven. There's a greater power in life and death."

"You sound like a rabbi. Or a priest."

"Well, you know I'm not either one. But now might be my turn to break some news to you."

"What news?"

"I accepted an invitation from your grandfather to go to Chicago for Thanksgiving."

"Okay, we'll go."

Martin smiled. "I can't believe you said yes just like that. I think I might be the one who's dreaming. I hadn't brought it up yet because I thought it would take a whole night of conversation to convince you."

Adam smiled as he walked closer to Martin and pinched his arm.

"Ouch."

"Guess you're not dreaming. We're going."

"What about Gabriella? Are you going to bring her too?"

"She'll be at the club for Thanksgiving with her parents, and she won't care. The way they do it there, it's like it's not even a holiday. It's like a business meeting with a backdrop of Thanksgiving. They won't even know I'm not there."

"Did your little dog friend already tell you that you should go to Chicago?"

"Not exactly, but I miss my grandfather. It's been too long."

"You could have gone with me for Yom Kippur."

"I just didn't feel like it."

"But now you do?"

Adam nodded. "I'll call tomorrow and let him know."

"No need. I already said yes for both of us."

"I'll get the tickets."

Martin reached inside a drawer and pulled out a pair of tickets. "Done."

* * *

After Martin left for his date, Adam decided to sit on the couch and rethink everything. He kicked off his shoes and took off his tie. He didn't like wearing ties daily, but his grandfather always told him that looking respectable goes a long way. He loved his grandfather, and some of his sayings and thoughts were embedded in Adam's head. The ties were a sign of respect for him. And it always felt good for Adam to stay on the straight and narrow, even if he occasionally slipped.

Adam knew that being raised by his grandparents was a lucky break. If his ass of a father had been in charge, who knows where he would have been? Probably not wealthy and successful.

He thought he should tell his grandfather about Gabriella, but he decided against it. He already knew she wasn't right for him; he didn't need Zach to tell him that.

Sometime after his last thought about Gabriella, Adam nodded off to sleep, hoping he would have some uninterrupted quiet.

He didn't see Gracie sitting on the chair across from him, nodding. Her plan was starting to jell.

Chapter Two

Zachary Feldman was so excited that Adam had agreed to come to Chicago for Thanksgiving. He immediately started writing a plan. Adam always liked to be in control of everything and Zach never wanted to rock the boat, but he knew he inevitably would.

Adam truly loved his grandfather and was always kind to him when they were together, so whatever damage Zach could have done was reversed, and they hugged and made up. Adam and Zach loved each other even when they didn't agree.

He missed his grandson more than ever and had grown accustomed to holidays without him. Even an occasional weekend would have been great, but Adam kept himself very busy with work because he didn't like dealing with anything sad or any unpleasant memories.

Adam never got over the fact that he didn't get to say goodbye to his grandmother before she died. She had a sudden heart attack, and he was so sorry about not visiting Chicago as much as he could have. He knew it was time to see his grandfather more, and he was determined not to miss this Thanksgiving dinner.

As for Zach, every Thanksgiving for as many years as he could remember, he hosted a party for his employees, especially those with no family. There was always a lot of food and laughter, but behind it all was a tinge of sadness because Adam chose not to come.

Zach promised himself that next time Adam came to town, he would find someone who was right for him. He knew that Adam had a lot of girlfriends for short periods, just for fun. Getting serious with one of them was not for him. Zach had met only a few because they never lasted long. He had no idea Adam was engaged. But even if he knew, he would still be hell bent on Adam coming back to Chicago.

This year, with Adam coming to Thanksgiving, Zach was going to celebrate even more than usual. When he got the call from Martin, he didn't let on that he had matrimony for Adam on his mind. He just felt great joy.

"Pops," Martin said, using the nickname he always called Zach. "The news is that we're coming. I can hardly wait."

There was a short silence on Zach's side of the conversation. "Whatever you did, thank you."

"What makes you think it was me?"

Zach laughed. "Because some things I just know. I need to say thank you one more time. Love you. You're a good boy. My second-favorite grandson."

"Pops, that works for me. This is going to be a great trip, and we're going to have a perfect Thanksgiving."

"No doubt. My boys will be in the house."

"See you soon. Can't wait for your cooking. I'm starved just thinking about it."

After the call was over, Zach felt like jumping up and down. Of course, if he did that, he might fall and break a bone. And then where would he be? He didn't want to spend Adam's visit in the hospital.

Gracie was standing behind him. "So, you're getting your wish. And so glad you decided not to jump up and down; who would run the deli?"

Zach laughed. "You would."

Gracie jumped up on the couch. "Let's discuss this like adults."

"You realize you're a dog, right?"

"I'm also a 100-percent real, state-of-the-art angel of romance."

"Did you know Adam was coming?"

"I sure did. You know I take my job very seriously. If I complete my assignment and everything goes as planned, I get to stay on Earth; if not, I'm homebound for a long while."

Zach shook his head in disbelief. "I feel like someone or something is taking control of me. A dog is controlling my life. Sorry, nothing personal."

"Let me stop you there, Zach. I'm not here to take over your life. I'm here because you made a wish a few months back, and I'm here to help. Once you get your wish, I'm gone. And don't think I don't know your little secret."

"What secret?"

"Your soup kitchen days."

"Are you going to tell me I'm too old?"

"No. I think it's good for you and the lovely people you serve."

"I suppose you know all my secrets."

"I do, but my lips are sealed. No worries, Zach. I know you're a good man, as is your grandson."

"You know Adam?"

"Of course. I've spent a lot of time with him. Sometimes he knew, but most of the time, I just observed his behavior. Everything he likes and dislikes, and I mean everything."

Zach didn't say much after that. He sat quietly, trying to understand all of this. If Adam had a chance to have a wonderful wife and family, that would be all Zach needed.

At his age, he should be on some fabulous island vacationing, relaxing, and having the time of his life. He tried it a few times over the last few years, but it wasn't exactly relaxing. He got so many phone calls that he had no time to take in the sights or meet people. The deli still needed him to ensure everything went right. And if he was honest with himself, Zach didn't think it was possible for him not to be there. He knew that would never actually happen while he was alive.

On some days, after the lunch crowd finished, he would tell everyone he was going home to get some rest. But he still wanted to do something. So, instead of resting, he volunteered at a soup kitchen in the city. That certainly kept him grounded. He loved talking to people and trying, in some small way, to help them—not only giving them food, but giving them hope. He often stayed to chat with a couple of the regulars and, when the day was over, he felt like he had accomplished something.

* * *

As Zach pulled up to the deli, he was happy to see a long line of customers waiting for dinner. He could have entered the back door, but he liked greeting everyone. He had done that for years, though he recently cut his hours. He was usually there for breakfast, lunch, and dinner, but sometimes headed out early when he thought he could get away. As his doctors reminded him too many times, even God rests.

The deli was bustling with people laughing and talking, a few loud babies cried, and plates clattered. It was quite a lively atmosphere. Some of the guests and staff were singing along with the background music Zach played in honor of his late wife. She loved music and decided it should always be playing in the background. Sometimes it was hard to hear because the deli was noisy, but Zach figured if a deli isn't noisy, it probably isn't good.

The shelves were filled with various kinds of mustards, ketchup, and hot sauces. The bagels and freshly baked bread scattered in bins smelled sensational. Jars of pickles rested on the counter, accompanied by giant forks to dig in and retrieve them.

Then there was the deli counter where customers picked up orders or waited for their food. The display was always as clean as a pin, but it got a bit messy closer to the back, where three people packed orders.

Zach spotted Molly out of the corner of his eye. She looked exactly like her photo. Her vibrant red hair was curly, and she was slender with green eyes and an innocent smile. She looked perfect for Adam; at least that's what Zach thought.

She moved toward him. "Hi, I'm Molly. Pretty crowded here."

"Thank goodness. I pray every night for customers to appear and guess what? They do. Anyway, I'm Zach." He held out his hand to shake hers. "So glad you came. I wasn't sure if I did the right thing."

"I wasn't sure I would come, but I was curious." His handshake made her feel comfortable. She was still questioning her decision, but she could always leave and forget this ever happened.

"Stay close," Zach said. "This is a hungry crowd, and they can get a little restless. Have a seat over there. I'll be there in a few minutes, just as soon as the crowd subsides. Oh, and please keep our arrangement between us. I didn't tell anyone about this."

Molly mimed zipping her mouth. "It doesn't seem like it will die down anytime soon."

"Just watch." Zach smiled and took out a whistle. Once he blew it, all was quiet. "My friends, hello to all. If we turn to our neighbors and smile at them, it will cause less chaos. While you're waiting, we'll pass out mini bagels, and everyone here tonight will receive a complimentary dessert. How does that sound?"

The crowd clapped and everything changed in a minute. People seemed satisfied with his offer. A little dessert never hurt.

When Molly arrived at the deli, she had noticed the strawberry cheesecake, a favorite of hers. It looked fabulous, and the pecan pie with whipped cream also looked inviting. She planned to get a piece before she left.

As she walked toward the booth where Zach told her to wait, Molly was stopped dead in her tracks by Madeline, an overweight woman with black glasses secured on her blonde and graying hair. The woman was holding menus and trying to speak to her.

"Missy, where are you going? We have a line. We follow the rules here." Her voice reminded Molly of a gym instructor she had at school—very firm and never nice.

"I have an appointment with Mr. Feldman. He just saw me and pointed to a booth in the back. He told me to wait there."

"Fine," she said. "He didn't tell me, but the old man never tells me anything."

"I guess I can understand that," Molly mumbled to herself.

"Did you say something? I didn't hear you."

"Nope. I didn't say a thing."

"I must have been mistaken. It's deafening in here. You know, a lot of people try to sneak past me."

"Well, just for the record, that's something I would never do."

Madeline took her menus and walked away in a huff.

Zach smiled when he sat down. "So, you've met Madeline. She's the drill sergeant here. Sometimes you need a person like that. If she goes over the top, we give her a day off. Madeline has worked here forever. My wife liked her, and I kept her on after she died. If she quit, I wouldn't be sad, but she's here until she isn't."

"Doesn't it bother you that she called you an old man?"

"No," Zach said with a laugh. "I am an old man. Now, let's start from the beginning. Hi, I'm Zachary Feldman." He reached out to shake her hand again.

"And I'm Molly Parker."

"I've never done anything like this before," Zach said. "I've heard about internet dating, but I felt like some kind of criminal putting my grandson's photo online and answering the questions as if I were him."

Molly smiled. "I doubt you were the only one who's ever done that. But you came clean, and that's why I'm here. Usually, when I visit those sites, I laugh and log off as quickly as possible. But after we talked, I thought you were doing something so lovely for your grandson that I wanted to meet you."

"I know I shouldn't have done this, but when we spoke, there was something about you that I thought was perfect for Adam. If you want to leave, I'll understand."

"I'm here, so give me a reason to stay."

"He's coming in for Thanksgiving. I want him to move back here, but I don't think he will do it just because I ask. I thought finding him a match might help."

"Maybe he feels like he's not marriage material."

"Have you ever been married?"

"No. I've been with the same man for years, and every time he asks me to marry him, I say no."

"Really? I don't get it. Why were you on the site? Do a lot of young people do things like that?"

"They sure do. They join these dating sites and hope for the best. They might like a partner, but marriage is not a must these days. You can have kids even if your relationship doesn't work."

"I guess I like the old way better, and I feel out of the loop."

"Look, what you're trying to do is admirable, but I'm sure your grandson can find his place in the world."

"He has found his place. It's just not here. And you? Have you found your place in the world?"

"My guy isn't the man for me. He's years older than I am and a good man, but we aren't the right blend."

"Maybe you'll fall madly in love with my grandson."

"I doubt it. And now that I'm here, to be honest, I have some questions."

"Let's get this party started. How can I help?"

"First, what's wrong with Adam? I'd like to know. Do I have anything to worry about?"

"Nothing is wrong with him; he just might need a little help picking out the right girl. Besides, he doesn't even live in Chicago."

"Where does this lover boy live?"

"New York City. But I always hope he'll move back here. I raised him and I miss him terribly. So, will you meet him?"

"I suppose so. Trust me, though, there is no way anything will ever happen with him. If that's alright with you, I'll do it."

"You never told me why you answered the ad."

"I don't know why. I just felt like seeing what would happen if I tried. I'm in a relationship, as I said before, but I'm not marrying him despite how he feels."

"Does he know that?"

"Yes, but he says he's not giving up on me."

"He seems like a nice guy."

"You're right, but I'm the problem. What about your grandson? Would he like this effort you're trying on his behalf?"

"He would probably hate it, but I don't know how to get my grandson to smell the roses before it's too late."

"Does he have a nice life in New York?"

"He says he does, but I'm not so sure. Luckily, he has his best friend with him. Martin. He takes care of everything, and Adam works all hours of the night."

"Do you think they might be—" Molly didn't even get to finish her sentence.

"Wait, you think they're gay? I wouldn't care if they were, but Martin was devastated after the loss of his wife; that's why he went to live with Adam. They're like brothers. Besides, it was very good for both of them. At least I didn't have to worry as much."

"Then you went online to find him a wife, and now I'm here?"

"Well, you might think I'm a little crazy, but I'm getting help from a friend. When you came up during my initial search for a match, she said you seemed perfect. Now that I've met you, I think she was right."

Molly had no idea why, but she decided to stay. She listened to Zach finish his story, never letting on that she felt something compelling the moment she entered the deli. It was getting busier by the moment, but Zach kept talking to her.

"So, Molly, what do you think? Can you hang around for a few minutes? I need to check on this hungry crowd."

"Sure thing."

Zach smiled at her. "I bet you're hungry."

"Starved is more like it."

"Are you going to stay for dinner?"

"I certainly am. Just for the record, I want to meet your grandson. We don't know each other well, but I see how much this means to you. I think I can meet him. No harm in that, right?"

Zach reached for her hand and gave it a good, solid squeeze. "Right. I feel like this is a good thing. You've made an old man very happy."

"No, I made Zach Feldman happy. What's age? Just a number."

"I used to say that when I was young. These days, it matters."

"From where I sit, you'll be here for a while. Doesn't seem like you're running out of steam. Your grandson's lucky to have you in his corner."

Zach was so happy at that moment. "Looks like my friend might have made a little magic happen."

"Can I meet your friend? Does she work here?"

"Not yet. She's not quite a deli worker." He wasn't about to tell her a dog started the ball rolling. She would think he was crazy. He thought he might be; listening to a dog still seemed a bit odd.

"Well, I, for one, love it here," Molly said. "It smells great, and it looks like a fun place to be. I haven't had fun for a long time, and that's something I miss. I didn't know until I walked in here that I needed more fun."

Zach smiled at his new friend. "We believe in fun. Everyone here works hard, but it's like a small family. We have fights, but they don't last long. We don't mix work with play, but all my employees have fun. That's a priority. If someone needs a day off, they cover for each other. If someone seems out of sorts, we try to help. All my employees have insurance and a profit-sharing plan. They're like my family."

By this time, Molly wanted to help make his dream come true. She wouldn't be falling in love with Adam—she was sure of that—but she felt a connection with Zach. He could be her grandfather, and she wished she had one like him. Her childhood wasn't great and she never knew her own grandparents, so Zach seemed like a perfect fit.

"Zach Feldman, I'm curious to meet this mystery man, your grandson. Can we talk more after dinner?"

"For sure. Everyone thinks better on a full stomach. I'll be back in a few minutes. Promise me you won't slip out?"

"I promise."

Zach looked toward the back of the deli, where Gracie was sitting. Zach waved to her and gave her the sign they agreed on earlier, saying that Molly might be the right choice. Gracie turned away and walked further into the back; a lot more needed to happen if they were going to get this right.

* * *

Zach wasn't easily impressed, but Molly was different. Adam's previous girlfriends were tall, beautiful blondes with model-like figures. They were like glamorous dolls with that faraway look in their eyes, hardly ever looking anyone in the eye. Zach agreed with Adam that they weren't marriage material; if he had married one of them, he would have been divorced by now. But then again, Zach might have gotten a great-grandchild in the deal. That was what Zach wanted, along with wanting his grandson to have a soulmate. Maybe that was selfish, but it was the truth.

Molly was slim, with dainty features. Her smile was genuine, her laugh was contagious, and her lashes were thick and long. Zach could tell that there was some sadness beneath her smile, but she was fascinating and the right girl for his grandson. Now all he had to do was figure out how they would meet.

He went back to his office to find Gracie. She was sitting at his desk, checking the computer while wearing his reading glasses.

"Zach, you'd better up your game or Molly will take a walk and probably never come back. You've got to win her over."

"I thought I did."

"Remember when I said this would be hard to do, but that you can't act desperate?"

Zach sat down on the chair beside her. "But I am desperate."

"Okay, then we need to adjust the plan. Your grandson will be here soon, so we need to have all hands on deck."

"We have a few days until he gets here."

"No, it's sooner than you think. He's going to surprise you."

"How do you know this?"

"Did you just ask an angel how I know something?"

"Fine. I'm with you. At least I'm trying to be, but I have to say this isn't easy."

"Zach, I apologize, but I'm a little testy because I don't want this to blow up in our faces. Anyway, I'm not sure when Martin and Adam will be coming here. I know Adam wants to spend a day or so downtown, but I'm pretty sure he won't be staying in the city."

Zach was caught totally off guard. "How do you know that?"

Gracie removed the glasses and put them down. "Listen, you must understand the players here. I know you, I know them, and I also know a few others who work here, plus Martin's life and dreams. This is my bonus job. I need to do this. Paris is my next stop if I succeed. If I don't, I'm not happy about my alternatives. We have work to do. Can you ask Molly to come back here?"

"Why? Maybe we should call the whole thing off." Zach shook his head, wondering if he should have done this a little slower. Or maybe not at all. He was worried that Adam would be upset. He might go back to New York and never talk to him again. Zach was mad at himself for pushing something he knew might be impossible. Sometimes a dream is just a dream. And a wish is just a thought.

Gracie looked at him and started to worry.

"I want to talk to Molly because she needs to stay in the loop. A lot will happen, and I want her to understand a few things."

"Okay. I'll get her, but I wish there was a way to put the genie back in the bottle."

"First, I'm not a genie; I'm an angel. Second, you can't stop believing. Just relax and let me think. Don't you have work to do? I know I do."

Zach left a little bit huffy, but Gracie knew he would get over it.

When Zach got to the table, Molly was buttoning her coat. She wasn't smiling, and Zach worried it was his fault. "Wait, are you leaving?"

"I think so. I can't imagine what I was thinking."

"Can you give me just a few more minutes? Someone wants to talk to you."

"Who here would want to talk to me?"

"Please, just for a minute. The friend I mentioned earlier? She's in my office and she wants to tell you some things."

Molly saw the desperation in his eyes and knew she couldn't just leave without doing one more thing for Zach. When Molly walked into his office, however, she didn't see anyone except a cute dog. She smiled and looked at Zach. "Now what?"

"When this conversation is over, we can talk. In the meantime, I'll get you some dinner. Then at least you won't feel like you came here for nothing."

"Zach it's okay. I should go. I never should have even been on the dating site. I keep thinking about what made me do such a crazy thing. I don't know you and you know nothing about me."

Then she heard a voice, and it wasn't Zach's. "Molly, have a seat. This won't take long. I promise. Perhaps this will make everything less confusing. I should have done this differently. My mistake."

"Done what differently? And who's talking?" All she saw a sweet-looking white and tan dog sitting behind the desk, wearing a pair of red reading glasses. When she turned around, she saw Zach had left, leaving just her and the dog. It was beginning to feel like a creepy movie.

"I'm Gracie," the dog said. "And yes, you watch too many creepy movies."

Molly thought she must be losing her mind. She was just a normal person with a normal life, and now she was talking to a dog in the back office of a deli.

"Is this one of those hidden-camera shows? The kind where you say, 'this can't be happening,' and they bring out a film crew, producers, and directors to yell 'surprise?'"

"This isn't anything like that. I'm a special angel. I'm here to grant your wish."

"I don't recall asking for help. I'm Molly Parker, and I think I've just lost my mind."

"You might think you don't need help, but you're looking for love in the wrong places." Gracie took off the glasses and gave Molly a straightforward stare.

"No, I'm just fine this way. I'm single. Never married, no children. Just me."

Gracie laughed. "Single? Didn't you forget Phillip?"

"How do you know about Phillip? This is getting creepy. I'm leaving."

"You don't have to leave. Nothing is going to happen to you. I know more about you than you think."

"Like what?"

"I knew you might need some proof, so here goes. When you were twenty, you went on a cruise with your aunt."

"Lucky guess. Lots of people go on cruises."

"They don't all fall in love with someone they met onboard and get married before they even dock. Ten days later, you were divorced. That's when you decided you would never get married again. But you're lonely and you asked for help."

Molly was too shocked to speak. Almost no one knew about her first marriage. Why would this little dog know anything about her?

Gracie could tell Molly wanted to leave but was curious enough to wait. "Do you need any more info before we get down to business?"

"No, because I'm not staying. We have never met and I'm sure all of this is for nothing. I'm going to go and pretend this never happened."

Gracie continued. "I see you need more info before you believe me. You like to know everything. You've been inquisitive since you were a young girl. Okay, remember the fountain? Buckingham Fountain on Michigan Avenue?"

"I love that fountain."

"I know that. You made a wish there that someday you would find someone who would understand you and love you for who you are."

"You have my attention. Go on. How do you know all this?"

"Honey, I was there."

"That's impossible. It was years ago."

"Molly, this is happening. You're here because a plan is in place. You can leave if you want, but the entire structure will be disrupted and many people will be unhappy."

"You mean meeting Zach the way I did was part of a plan?"

"Yes, but not a good one."

Molly laughed, feeling a bit more comfortable. "You think?"

"I know. Even though I thought I knew everything about you, I was not the first angel coming down to help. She's on leave."

"On leave? What does that mean?"

"Never mind about her. She had to return to the training lab, and it takes a long time to retrain. It's now my job to fix this. And I will. I'm not entirely sure where we go from here, but I'm in the process of making a new plan. So, bear with me and be patient. Everything will be as it should."

"What if I don't want to be here?"

"You can go but we both know your life is very empty because of your fears. Good things happen to good people. That's why we're here having this discussion. I'm an angel, not a devil."

"Sure. You're an angel and I'm a rock star making millions."

"If you give me a chance to explain things, maybe you'll feel better. I know it's not your style. Just trust me."

Molly sat down and took a few deep breaths. She always took time to rethink when she got nervous. Gracie knew that Molly never liked surprises; she couldn't let her sit there worried.

"Molly, let me give you the rundown. This was supposed to be seamless, but it's not. Remember when you moved in with Phillip?"

"Of course I do. I had no job, no money, and not much of a family left."

"You had a job. You were a teacher—a great one. After you left, the entire staff was devastated. And the kids were so sad."

"I had no idea. I just left and no one called me back."

"Of course you didn't. You never look back. One of my plans—and don't say no when you hear it—is for you to return to the classroom. I know you've been thinking about it."

Molly was finally beginning to realize that Gracie could at least read minds. Or maybe she really was an angel.

"You seem to know quite a bit about me. So why didn't you help me move forward with Phillip?"

"That one's simple. He isn't your destiny."

"How do you know that?"

"You realize you've been dodging Phillip's proposals for quite a long time. He's a wonderful guy. Either you don't understand what love is or you know he's not right for you."

"I don't know what answer you're looking for."

"There's no right or wrong answer. Unless I'm wrong, you're not in love with him."

"Phillip seems to think things are good the way they are," Molly responded, realizing she had never thought about it that way. "Maybe they are."

"He wants a stable life and you're not ready for that if it's going to be with him. Why do you think you were looking for love on the internet?"

"I don't know. It was a mistake."

"No, it wasn't. You wouldn't have met Zach otherwise. Now we have a lot of work to do. I promise you that everything will work out, but I can't tell you more. I've already overplayed my hand."

"I'm so confused. You're a dog, you're talking to me, and I'm just supposed to follow your lead. Right?"

"Now that's the Molly I know and love. Go get a seat at the deli, have a great dinner, and pretend we never talked. I'll take care of the rest. That's my job. If this doesn't work out,

I won't be allowed to stay. I will have to go back to heaven. Not that heaven isn't beautiful, but I love it here on Earth."

"Before I go back out, I have a question. I have a lot of them, but this one matters most."

"Okay, one question."

"You seem to know so much about me. Have you been with me since birth?"

"No, that was the angel who got reassigned. I took over when you were in grammar school, but I've read your history and know everything about you. You're a good person, and you'll be happy. I can promise you that."

Molly sat there for a few minutes, feeling like she had been hit by a brick. "I believed in angels, but this is so far out of my realm. I don't really like discussing my life with anyone."

"I'm not just anyone. You need to think of me as a friend. I have your back; just stay with me. Zach is a good man, and I can see he likes you. Let's give him his wish."

* * *

Molly took a couple of deep breaths, went back to the table, and sat across from Zach. She took her coat off and was smiling, which Zach thought meant good news. He was hesitant to ask any questions, but he wanted to hear what Molly had to say about Gracie.

"Are you in?" he finally asked.

"That depends."

"On what?" Zach was prepared to offer her almost anything.

"Are you going to feed me? I told you I'm starved. Besides, it might be bad luck to ignore an angel."

They both laughed, realizing that whatever happened next, they were now in it together.

"If you're hungry, let's eat," Zach said. "Food heals everything."

They chatted for more than an hour, talking between bites of matzo ball soup, corned beef, and the best fries Molly had ever eaten. It was perfect comfort food.

Molly was impressed by Zach's kindness and could see why the deli was so successful. Madeline interrupted them several times because she wanted to know everything that was happening, but Zach kept her in the dark. She was quite the gossip.

Molly was full, but she had one more thing in mind.

"Zach, could I get a piece of strawberry cheesecake? It looked so good."

"It's even better than it looks."

After coffee and dessert, they continued their talk. By this time, the staff was growing interested in Molly. Zach knew he'd need to reassure them she wasn't going to be their new boss. He knew from experience that whenever he had a private conversation, everyone wondered if he was selling and retiring.

"How would you like to be the hostess for just a few days?"

"I assume you mean just until Adam leaves."

"Exactly."

"What about Madeline?"

"I'll give her a few days off. She won't mind. So, you'll do it?" Zach asked while crossing his fingers under the table. He saw Gracie observing from the back before she nodded and disappeared.

"You had me at the chopped liver," Molly said. "I will do what I can to help you. But you should know why; it's because I liked you from the minute we met. I felt like I had known you forever. Isn't that crazy?"

"No, I get it. I still believe in miracles. So, you'll meet Adam?"

"I will. If he's anything like you, this might be fun. I thought the way you handled the crowd was extraordinary. When I walked in, I looked around and fell in love with this place."

"There are days when nothing clicks, but usually everything works."

"It looks challenging but interesting. I could use a job that's different than my regular life. I'm not afraid of change. Change is good; it keeps people on their toes."

"I can guarantee it'll be different. Have you ever worked in a restaurant?"

"Kind of, a long time ago. I've never cooked but I could try. It might be kind of funny."

"That's okay," Zach said. "I'm not looking for a cook. I have enough employees and my staff luckily doesn't take much time off. So, you're in?"

"I'm in. I think you and I are going to have a great relationship. But remember, that doesn't mean your grandson and I are a match."

"You never know. You might be."

"Well, then," Molly held out her hand. "Can we shake on this? I have no expectations other than working here and having a good time."

"Let me give you a tour and you can meet everyone. The dinner rush is almost over—"

"Why don't you show me around tomorrow? And just for the record, I want to be treated like everyone else... Speaking of that, what should I call you?"

"Just Zach. That's what everyone calls me to my face; what they call me anywhere else is up to them." He laughed. "I'm joking. My crew is one terrific bunch and I'm nothing without them."

"I don't know about that. I think you've got a heart of gold."

"Don't tell anyone. I'll lose my quiet power."

Molly laughed. "Oh, I think they know who the boss is. I've been watching."

Zach was pleased with their plan. As he walked Molly to the door, he held her hand tightly. "I probably shouldn't say this, but you're so impressive. I know you're not interested in getting married, but please just be open minded when you meet Adam. That's all I ask."

"I promise to be fair."

"I know I can be intense—"

"That's one of your charms," Molly added as she waved goodbye and walked out the door.

Zach opened the door a crack and shouted back. "I didn't even know I had charms."

"You do." And then she smiled and walked out. Molly couldn't help but feel overwhelmed; it had been quite a day. She had no idea what was going to happen, but she was sure she would keep her guard up.

Success, Zach thought as he watched Molly walk away. Then he looked up and thought about Dora. He missed his wife and sometimes felt her spirit was still with him and watching. Zach was always in awe of her. Unlike his grandson, who always believed that everything would work out, Zach had always been a worrier. He hoped Dora would approve of his plan—and wondered whether it would work.

* * *

When Zach got home, Gracie was already there to greet him. He was glad he had asked Charlotte, one of his star employees, to take her home while he finalized the deal with Molly.

"How did it go?"

"She agreed to meet Adam and to work at the deli for a little while. Still, I feel like there's something I'm missing."

"You're not missing anything. You started the ball rolling, and we have a very complicated mission ahead of us."

"Are we doing the right thing?" Zach asked. "Molly is a sweet person, and I don't want her to get hurt."

"Of course. You love your grandson, and you want him to be happy. How could that be a mistake? You've been asking for something like this for years. Trust me; we're good at what we do. Believe me, we do our research. I can't promise you it always works out, because sometimes it doesn't. But it does most of the time."

"What happens if it doesn't?"

"We fix it. We have a lot of angels in heaven, so no need to worry. If we're not up to par, we go back to school. We don't get sent down until we're tested and we pass."

Zach headed to his bedroom, but Gracie followed him still talking.

"I want you to understand this. Sometimes you might think we don't hear you. Heaven is a long way up, but we get the message loud and clear. Molly, Adam, and you were all constantly wishing for happiness. You wanted this, so let me do my job. Please."

"In other words, I don't have any control about what happens next."

"I hate to put it this bluntly, but yes. What happens next isn't a question of control."

"What do I do now?" Zach asked, pretty sure there was no answer.

"Humans are always looking for something or someone to make them happy, but it's not our job to wave a magic wand and say everything will be fine. Our job is to help. We're helpers. We do what we can."

After saying goodnight, Zach closed the bedroom door behind him. What he didn't know was Gracie sat on the chair beside him all night long.

Chapter Three

Molly decided to arrive early at the deli so she could get a feel for everything. She also wanted to meet the staff, and Zach had agreed that the morning would be a good time. He was waiting for her at the door.

"No need to park that far away from the restaurant," he said. "A car is just a car. I'm not hiring you because you lack financial resources and need a job. I'm hiring you because I like you and I want my grandson to meet you."

Molly smiled. "Thanks. You know this whole thing is a little scary for me because—"

Zach finished her sentence. "Because you haven't worked in a restaurant in a long time. You told me that already. Don't worry; I have you covered. Madeline was happy to have a few days off. I'm sure you'll do great."

"Thanks for the vote of confidence." Molly was pleased that he viewed her that way, but she couldn't help but think about what could wrong. A whole lot of scenarios were tossing around in her brain, but that didn't stop her from showing up.

"Zach, maybe I should address you as Mr. Feldman. I think that would be better. I'm working here, and I should show respect."

"Nonsense. Like I said, everyone calls me Zach."

Suddenly, two guys burst straight out of the kitchen arguing at the top of their lungs.

Zach immediately took charge. "Hey, you two, what gives?"

They turned to him and continued arguing.

"Hold on, you're talking too fast," he told them. "I can't understand this."

"Sorry, Zach," the first man said. "This meatball head told me to cook faster. I cook fast, but he likes me to do it faster. What does he know? He has no clue how to make meatballs."

"Okay, stop for a second," Zach said. "Meet Molly. She's pinch-hitting for Madeline. Molly, meet Willis and Enrico. They're always on each other's cases, but we understand. Sometimes we take bets on who wins. Right, guys?"

They laughed it off, but Zach could sense a little more tension than usual.

Enrico was an incredible chef, and a very handsome Italian man with a strong accent. Willis was born and raised in Paris and was over-the-top talented. He created bakery goods fit for royalty.

"Hi," Molly said in a quiet voice. "Nice to meet you."

Zach whispered to Molly, "You've got to talk louder, or this place will eat you up. It's a deli on steroids. Also, see, everyone calls me Zach just like I said. You can do the same."

Enrico and Willis stopped fighting, smiled, and shook hands. Then, just as they always did, they walked back to the kitchen with their problem unresolved. Some days they seemed to pick fights just to make their morning more exciting; Zach noticed they always cooked better on those days.

"What just happened?" Molly asked. "Will they continue the argument or forget about it?"

"They'll probably continue, but it will be subdued. In a few hours, they'll act like it never happened at all. Come on, let me introduce you to the rest of the Feldman family."

Zach moved through the deli with Molly by his side. He sometimes took chances when it came to hiring, but some of the staff had now been with him for more than twenty years; he was doing something right.

Leo was in the back, sorting silverware and singing along with the oldies station playing in the background. He was one of the best servers the deli had. He never got an order wrong.

"Leo, meet Molly. She'll be helping with reception and special events. Molly, Leo is a master of tai chi. Sometimes when we have a rough day here, he leads a few minutes of mind and body healing."

"Sounds like a terrific idea," Molly said.

"Do you do tai chi?" Leo asked. He had a warm smile to go with his perfect build.

"As a matter of fact, I do," Molly said. "It calms me when I get over the top."

Leo nodded, thinking Zach might have found a diamond in the rough. He pulled Zach aside. "Good pick spiritually, my friend. I have a feeling you have a plan. I don't know what it is, but I have a feeling it will be successful. Is this about Adam?"

"Could be," Zach said. "How do you know?"

"I can feel the vibe. She's got that vibe."

"You approve?"

"I have a good feeling about this."

Zach smiled. "Me too." He crossed his fingers, said goodbye, and took Molly to meet the others.

"Next, we'll meet the deli geniuses. These guys are terrific. We have a lot of customers who aren't sweet, and some are downright rude. Nowadays, people are in a hurry and don't want to wait for anything. But my guys can handle them. Molly, meet Morry, Nathan, and Geraldine."

Morry was short and pudgy. He had a fabulous personality; everyone loved him and his jokes. Nathan was tall, lanky, and very experienced. He could cut deli meat with his eyes closed. Geraldine was a plain and simple woman who never forgot anything. She made sure every order was packed just right.

Even though it was still early in the morning, they were already swamped with orders, so Zach decided to let them get on with their work. When they got a bit overwhelmed, Zach would roll up his sleeves and help anytime.

Molly watched Zach grab salami sticks for two of them. "This is the best of the best—spicy and very tasty. I have broken a tooth or two, but it's worth it. Want one?"

She held up her hand. "Not my thing."

"Once you work here for a while, it might become your thing."

"I won't be here that long. Plus I'm more of a bologna girl. I like it thin sliced, soft, and on rye."

"We've got that too. A girl after my own heart."

They both laughed.

"I taught Adam how to cut deli meat. Him and his best buddy, Martin. I taught them both years ago, just in case something happened to me. Martin's a pro; he could run this place. Adam probably could too, but he never would."

As they walked toward a booth to discuss some details, Zach let Molly in on the importance of the team she had just met. "Without these guys, there would be no deli."

"Do they all get along?"

"Not always. They fight sometimes. But we follow the old rule that if a couple fights, they should make up before they go to bed."

"I've heard that. I think it's kind of cute."

"Good, because that's what we do here. No one leaves mad at the end of the day. By the time they come in the next day, they've forgotten about it. That's what family does."

Molly couldn't believe what a lucky break it was for her to meet Zach. She didn't know anyone like him—which made her wonder why his grandson didn't visit more regularly.

* * *

Gracie watched as everything took its course. Things were going according to plan, but she knew something could come undone when there were this many players involved.

Later that morning, she realized there was a bit of a hiccup.

The lunchtime rush had just started. And Gracie saw a woman standing in the doorway, waiting to enter. Gracie had no idea who she was, but she was gorgeous, tall, and blonde. She looked like she was in the wrong place.

Molly was at the hostess station and approached the woman first. "How many will there be?"

"I'm just waiting."

"You can sit at a table. When they come, I'll send them over."

"I'm not staying. I'm looking for Adam Feldman. Is he here?"

"I haven't seen him," Molly said. "But I'll seat you close to the door. When he comes, I'll send him your way."

"Fine." Her tone was not enthusiastic.

"His grandfather's in the back. Should I get him?"

"That would be great."

"Who should I say is looking for him?"

"I'm Gabriella, Adam's fiancée. I came to surprise him."

At that moment, Molly wanted to get her coat, walk out, and never come back to the deli. She felt her heart racing; at the same time, a surge of jealousy washed over her. That was strange because she still hadn't even met Adam.

Gabriella stepped outside, motioning for her driver to wait. That gave Molly a chance to ask Charlotte what she should do.

"Adam's fiancée is here," she whispered.

"What are you talking about?" Charlotte asked. "He doesn't have a fiancée."

"That's who she said she was. She didn't seem like the joking type."

Charlotte was quick on her feet and knew she should be the one to handle this.

"Molly, I got this. You can finish whatever you were doing."

"Good idea. I'll go get Zach."

"Perfect."

While Molly went to the back, Charlotte sprang into action.

"Hi, I'm Charlotte. Nice to meet you."

Gabriella didn't respond at first. She just stood there looking around, seeming anxious and uncomfortable. Then she asked, "Is he here?"

"Who?"

"Adam Feldman. I need to speak to him right now."

"You can talk to his grandfather. I'll grab him from the back."

"Thank you," Gabriella answered, wanting to get out of there as quickly as she could.

"How about some coffee or water?" Charlotte asked, hoping she said no because she didn't want to serve her. "Or we have several types of tea."

Gabriella looked around, feeling awkward. She had no idea that Adam's grandfather owned a deli; she'd always assumed it was a fine dining restaurant like the kind they ate at when they weren't at the club. "No, I'm fine."

Charlotte wondered what was taking Zach and Molly so long, though she knew Adam's engagement would be shocking news.

By the time Zach eventually walked over to the booth, Gabriella had left. Zach figured it was probably for the best, but he wondered why he hadn't known about her. He would wait for an explanation from Adam—and it had better be a good one.

Chapter Four

Adam missed several things about Chicago, including the pizza. There was nothing like a Gino's or Lou Malnati's deep-dish pizza—not to mention Gibson's, the most excellent steakhouse ever. New York had some terrific restaurants that Adam loved, but Chicago was in his blood even if he pretended it wasn't. On occasion, he thought about moving back but never told anyone that—not even Martin. If it were up to Martin, they would have moved back a few years ago.

A few minutes into the flight to Chicago, Adam was sound asleep. As usual, once he closed his eyes it wasn't easy to wake him. Martin sometimes needed to splash water on Adam to get him up in the morning.

Though they traveled first class, Martin was the only one eating, even if he wasn't sure he could keep it down. No matter how hard he tried, he couldn't fall asleep. He wanted to make sure he would up and ready to go if something happened; he didn't want to sleep through a crash. Dramamine didn't work for Martin, and even a few drinks didn't help. He just sat upright, holding the armrests tightly and counting the minutes until the plane touched down. He long ago accepted that he would never like flying; he always wished Adam would opt for a train or driving instead.

The flight attendant kept a close eye on him; she knew a nervous flyer when she saw one. "So, Mr. Jacobs, how are you doing?"

"So far, so good. If there's no turbulence, all will be well." He was already holding the bag from the seat in front of him, just in case things turned rocky.

"This flight is a short one," she said. "So there's no need to worry. I'll keep an eye on you."

"From your mouth to God's ear," Martin added, thinking he might be a little chattier if they were anywhere other than on a plane.

Moments later, the attendant returned with some ginger ale and crackers. "This might help."

"Great." He smiled as he poured some into a small cup left over from his meal. "It'll help; it always does."

"I just checked with the pilot. According to him, everything is in order. The weather pattern is not complicated, and the flight isn't long. Sit back, close your eyes, and you'll be in Chicago before you know it."

The flight attendant was beautiful, with long legs, blonde hair, and a short, tailored skirt paired with a button-down, fitted jacket that showcased her figure. Martin might have asked for her phone number in a bar, but he was too preoccupied to do that on the plane.

Martin's only priority was to land safely; nothing else mattered. He was happy to talk with the attendant so he would know if there was a problem, but nothing would change the fact that he was a nervous flyer.

Later, when they were preparing for the landing, the flight attendant dropped her card in his lap. "If you're in Chicago for a while, call me. I'll be back the day after tomorrow."

When he didn't respond, she tried to take the card back. "I'm sorry I misjudged." She pointed to Adam. "I understand if you have a boyfriend."

Martin laughed. "Oh, we're not a thing. We've been best friends since we were kids. I take care of his apartment, cook, clean, and handle his social calendar. We're going to his grandfather's house for Thanksgiving. When we were kids, we always said that whoever made more money would help the other one. He wound up with the money, plus the brains and the looks."

"You seem pretty perfect to me," she replied.

He blushed a bit and smiled. "Thanks. Nice of you to say that. I'm more the rugged type. I used to climb, and one of my favorite things was walking the trails, but that was years ago. I'm not in the best of shape now, but I'll get there."

"I'm sure you will, honey." She smiled mischievously, hoping he would call. That was how she entertained herself in different cities and countries.

Martin knew he had no intention of calling her. Being catered to on a plane relaxed him, and he still liked flirting with attractive women, but he wasn't looking for anything new. Still, he took the card and put it in his pocket.

When the seatbelt light came on and they were almost ready to land, Martin nudged Adam. "Time to get up."

Adam smiled. "I woke up in time to catch the end of that. You know, anywhere we go you always get the most gorgeous girl to ask you out. How do you do it?"

"I don't know, but it helped me get through the flight. You know I don't like flying."

As they walked off the plane, Martin winked at Adam. "I still have pretty good game, wouldn't you say?"

"I think I have you beat," Adam pushed back.

"What? Getting engaged to someone you don't love without even telling your grandfather? That's a good game?"

"Fine, you win. I'll tell my grandfather when we get to his house tomorrow. In the meantime, let's have fun like we used to. This is our hometown."

"Glad you remembered. I was beginning to think you would never come back. Any chance you'd considering moving back here?"

"Yes and no, depending on how this visit goes. I haven't spent much time with my grandfather lately. I want to spend time with him and share the joy and laughter that life offers before it's too late."

"I can't believe this is you talking."

"Maybe I had an epiphany in a dream."

"Maybe so, but have you talked to Gabriella about it? You do remember that you're engaged, right?"

"I'll just break the engagement. You know I'd never make it down the aisle. I doubt Gabriella will care."

"Why would you say that? She said yes. She's probably got the whole thing planned."

"If it's planned, her mother did it," Adam replied. "Her mother is involved in every step of her life. It'd be like marrying both of them—probably another wedding at the club that feels more like celebrating a business contract. I created this monster, so I'll have to dismantle their whole idea of a beautiful socialite wedding."

"I'd wondered if she ever asked if she could meet your family. Did you even mention you have a grandfather and a whole bunch of people in Chicago who love you? Or did you forget about them?"

"Of course I did. She wasn't interested in hearing much about it, but he raised me and I love him."

"Maybe you should tell him that."

"I hope he knows I love him. It would be terrible if he didn't."

"Yes, it would. Maybe you should make sure to tell him on this trip."

"I will. And when we get back to New York, I'll break it off with Gabriella."

"Did you ask her to come?"

"No. I thought about it but decided not to."

"And she never asked you why you were going to Chicago?"

"Not that I remember. I'm sure Gabriella will have a lovely Thanksgiving with her family. They all sit at the table and don't talk to each other. I'm not sure she ever has fun unless she's watching her soap operas."

"Not a great life for anyone," Martin said, wondering if Adam would really break up with her.

"She is beautiful—"

Martin laughed. "There's more to life than just beautiful women."

"I sincerely hope so."

"Take it from me. You will find happiness, though it might look different than what you expect."

"Now, let's forget about Gabriella and have a great week. It's just us, and we're here for a good time."

Chapter Five

The restaurant was so busy that Molly didn't have much time to think about how she got there in the first place. Not until her lunch break later in the day, when she pretended to read a book while her thoughts wandered.

As a young girl, she read all the romance books she could get her hands on. When she was older, she re-read them, realizing the impossibility of finding her own Prince Charming and questioning whether she even cared about that.

She knew that if she wanted to get married, all she had to do was say yes. Phillip Wainwright was a successful and distinguished older man who loved her. She liked him very much and enjoyed spending time with him, but she didn't love him—at least not in the way she wanted.

She moved into Phillip's home after a few months of dating and only a couple of kisses here and there. He promised not to rush her. He always hoped she would say yes to one of his proposals, but her answer was always the same—"we'll see." He kept the ring, ten carats of breathtaking emerald-cut diamond, in his sock drawer. He hoped he would win her over someday. He could give her a great life if only she would let him.

When Molly saw his home for the first time, she was overwhelmed by its magnitude. A grand staircase led to eight bedrooms, each with a private bath and sitting room. To make it even more elegant, each bedroom had a private balcony. Every room was different, yet perfectly adorned with lovely furniture, accessories, plants, and state-of-the-art technology.

Everything in the house was warm and comfortable. She enjoyed living there, and Phillip was such a great guy. She took him up on sharing his life and his home, but marriage was too much for her. She explained that to Phillip when she agreed to move in, but he was so in love with her he agreed to whatever she wanted, hoping the day would come when she changed her mind.

His beautiful home didn't reflect the way he ran his life. He felt a responsibility to care for others who might be less fortunate and was giving in the most wonderful ways. Phillip had been married three times but never had children. With Molly, he wanted it all: a large wedding, a beautiful honeymoon, and kids.

* * *

When Molly got home that night, Phillip looked pale and anxious. She could tell he'd been pacing, wondering when she would return. Molly rarely left the house for long, but she had been gone most of the last several days.

"What in the world happened to you?" he asked her. "I asked Harrison to stay because I thought I might need him."

Harrison had been with Phillip for years. Not only was he head of the security team, but he had become a good friend.

Molly walked over and kissed Phillips's forehead. "Just needed some time. Don't be mad. I'm fine. I should have called."

She couldn't very well tell him the truth. Why would she be on one of those internet dating sites? She had him. Wasn't that enough?

"You could always have Harrison take you wherever you want to go," Phillip said.

"I know, but driving is relaxing." Molly also never minded riding the bus because it kept her focused on her life before she met Phillip.

"Honey, if you want space, just tell me. I want you to be happy. I'm not mad. I could never get mad at you."

"Good, then be happy for me. I got a job at a restaurant."

"A job? What on Earth for? You can have anything you want. Just say the word and it's yours."

"I know that, but I like to get out and do things. I enjoy having my own money and getting up every day to go somewhere."

Phillip looked disappointed. "Does that mean you're leaving me?"

She smiled and shook her head. "It's just a job."

The truth was that, after meeting and getting to know Zach, she was becoming excited to meet Adam. That realization shocked her. Finding out he had a fiancée was disappointing, of course, but everything that had happened lately was strange and confusing. She decided to go with the flow and see what happened. After all, she knew little about Adam other than he had a wonderful grandfather.

At this point in her life, not much interested her. Some days she didn't even want to get out of bed. Her curiosity about Adam was a welcome feeling.

"Molly, please think about what your life could be like if you married me."

"I will, but please let me just breathe a little for now. I know you mean well, but right now I need time."

Phillip knew her well enough to end that part of the conversation. He had asked her to marry him many times already and would keep trying, hoping one day the answer would be yes.

"I know I promised you I wouldn't talk about it," Phillip said. "I'll drop it for now. Promise."

Molly couldn't let Phillip take the blame. "I'm so sorry. I should have called. This is my fault. I was inconsiderate. Please accept my apology."

"Oh, sweetie. It's not you. It's me. I think I'm getting a bit insecure."

She laughed. "You insecure? No way."

"Yes, it's true." Then he took her by the hand. "Let's go watch a movie."

"Good idea. It's been a long day."

Molly wondered what Phillip would have said if he really knew what was going on. She knew all the details, and she was beginning to think this was all a dream. Even though Phillip had changed the subject, she had a few things to add.

"I know you want me to go to the country club, spend time with your friends, and accompany you to social events."

"Of course I would like that."

"It's just not for me. You know I'm so different from your friends and their wives."

"I know that. I'm sorry. It's wishful thinking but I get it. I really do."

Neither of them could see her, but Gracie was watching. She was hoping they would wrap up their conversation but, as usual, it kept going even though they had both agreed to stop.

"I go to the club because some of these guys have been my friends for years," Phillip said. "If I just left them out in the cold, it would be a bad blow to all of them."

"They're your friends, not mine. I don't really know them."

"You could try. Maybe you just need some time to get used to this kind of life."

"I don't know; it's just not me. I hate the gossipy part of the club."

"Okay, I get it. Work wherever you want. I'll be here waiting. Maybe you'll come to your senses. It's hard working in a restaurant."

"What makes you say that?"

"My first job was in a restaurant. I washed dishes. I even won a contest."

"You never mentioned that before."

"We had a bet every week on which of us would wash the most dishes. That made the job go faster and seem less boring."

"I had no idea." Phillip and Molly rarely talked about their lives before they met.

"It's not something I think about too often, but it's a part of me. It's part of why I support six food banks in the Chicagoland area and replenish many of the soup kitchens. I know how hard that work can be."

Molly was interested in hearing more, but Phillip stopped as though he had shared too much.

"I hope you still have time to spend with me," Phillip confessed.

"It's only for a little while. I'll be home every night. I love living here. You know that."

"I do, but I want to share everything with you."

"You're such a good man. And now that I know some of the wonderful things you do, I'm impressed."

"I didn't tell you to impress you. I hope you know that loving you has been the best part of our time together. If you decide to stay, I will be thrilled. If, in time, you don't, I will try to understand. Just know I'm patient. At least tell me where you're working."

"Hello Deli. In Skokie."

"You're kidding?"

"No, I'm just looking for something completely different from what I'm used to."

"Well, I've got to give you that. It's different, alright. I always figured if you got a job, it would be something related to your master's. Remember how hard you worked to get it?"

"Yes, can't forget that," she said sarcastically. She had almost dropped out about ten times, but she managed to complete her studies. "I have other dreams. The ones I don't talk about."

"I'm sure you do. You've got your whole life ahead of you."

"I know that. I also know how much you've given me. You've been generous, kind, and very loyal."

Phillip laughed. "You make me sound like a dog."

"That's not what I meant."

"You must know the boss at the deli, Zach Feldman. He helps out at the soup kitchen. He's one of the good guys."

She smiled. "Good to know."

Phillip was happy to see her smile. "Don't forget, I want to help you. So just know that."

"I know you do, but it's been hard for me. My life story isn't pretty. I guess after my mom died, I never got over being alone. My father was still alive and could have helped me, but he didn't. I needed him, and he just left."

"That doesn't mean you can't allow yourself to be happy."

"I feel lucky that you're here for me. The only other person in my life was my aunt. She came to my rescue just like you did. I could never repay you for all you've given me."

"You don't need to repay me. I just want to look at you and see that some of the pain is gone. If I can't be the one to do that for you, I will be happy if someone else can. You deserve it."

Phillip smiled as he looked at Molly. She was so beautiful, and people noticed her when she walked into a room. She still had that effect on him. And even if she didn't love him the way he loved her, that was enough for him.

"Okay, go have fun." He knew how much he would miss her while she was working, but having her sometimes was better than not having her at all. "I know in my heart you'll come home to me one day and say, 'It's time.' And then when we're old and gray, we'll look back and laugh."

"You might be right."

"Just hurry up. I'm not getting any younger."

"Maybe not," she said. "Ready to go upstairs?"

Phillip took her in his arms and hugged her affectionately, knowing that she was the only woman for him.

"Phillip, you're wonderful, but—"

"Let's forget the buts for tonight. Positive thoughts would be nicer. Let's pretend we have no problems. Those can wait until tomorrow."

She smiled. "Okay, I promise. Let's go up and watch a movie. You can pick, because I'll probably be asleep before the movie even starts."

Molly never understood how a man like Phillip could be interested in her. She didn't accomplish anything important. She'd graduated college and finished a master's degree in education, and that still wasn't enough for her to think she could have a successful future. She doubted herself at every turn. Her romantic life was no different, but maybe things were changing.

Chapter Six

Adam and Martin were waiting for their luggage when a message came over the loudspeaker. "Flight 333 has had a baggage delay. We're trying to resolve it as quickly as possible."

About thirty minutes later, the crowd of angry faces around the luggage carousel received an update. "We apologize for the inconvenience, and we're doing everything we can to assist you. Baggage delivery will be available in an hour or two. Please line up at gate six. We will provide vouchers for food while you wait and notify you of updates as soon as possible."

Amid the whistles and many boos, Adam whispered to Martin, "Let's get out of here. I rented a car this time."

Martin couldn't help but be amused. "A car?"

Adam expected the question because he hadn't driven himself anywhere for years. "I just felt like it. I rented a red

Porsche. You know I always wanted one since I was a teenager, but I never had anywhere to drive one in New York. The traffic is much easier here."

"Unless it's construction season." Martin laughed, knowing better than his friend what a nightmare Chicago traffic could be. "What about our luggage?"

"Time for some new clothes." Adam started moving through the crowd toward the exit.

"You're kidding, right?"

"Follow me. Let's have some fun. This is Chi-town."

Martin was shocked but happy. He saw some of his best friend's old personality coming through. It had been a long time since he had seen him so happy, and he hoped it would last.

"I can drive if you want," Martin suggested.

"This is a rental, and I want to bring it back in one piece."

"Okay, you're the boss."

They laughed, looking forward to the change of coming home. New York was a great place to live, but Chicago was still home.

Adam's excitement at driving a Porsche disappeared when they got to the rental office and saw the sign hanging on the door: *We apologize but there are no cars available due to rapid turnover of inventory. No rentals are available today. Your money has already been refunded.*

Adam was disappointed, but he made a call and, a few minutes later, the two of them were in a luxury limousine with a small minibar in the back.

Martin smiled. "You seem to be taking this with a grain of salt."

"No problem. Once we get some new clothes, I'll get us a car—or better yet, we'll continue with a driver. Guess me driving a Porsche is not in the cards."

"Sounds like a plan," Martin said, opening a can of 7-Up. "Want one?"

"Sure do. I'm feeling pretty good being here."

"Let's call your grandfather."

"Not yet. Let's get some clothes and let the chips fall as they may."

"Maybe they'll find our luggage."

"And maybe they won't. Who cares? Let's just eat and then we'll see. No problem either way."

Martin put his hand on his buddy's head. "Do you have a fever or something?"

Adam laughed. "Just feeling free with no cares. I'm open to fun and a free schedule. There are no meetings or important phone calls. Just what I needed."

"Are you sure you didn't hit your head or something?"

"No, just rethinking the future."

"If you're not happy with the path you chose, you can always make some changes."

Adam shrugged. "I don't know. Some days I think about changing things, but then I check my bank account. It looks good to me."

"Look, we've been friends forever. If you're unhappy, we can change everything. I have no ties to any place; there's nothing holding me anywhere. But you, my friend, are still engaged. I don't think I need to remind you about that decision."

"I know. I made that one myself. Sometimes I wonder how I got so rich; I've made pretty bad decisions once or twice."

Martin gave his buddy a look. "Once or twice?"

"Maybe too often to count."

Martin didn't say anything. It was no secret that he didn't like Gabriella, but the decision was ultimately up to Adam. The good news was Adam was talking like there might be some changes in the future.

Martin knew Adam loved his grandfather and it might be good for Adam and Zach to have some time together. Zach wasn't getting any younger. Martin's own grandparents had passed away before he could remember anything about them. He wished he had a grandfather like Zach and knew he had been lucky to be Adam's best friend. Zach couldn't have loved Martin any more if he were blood. Blood is blood, but love trumps all.

Adam changed the subject. "Are you hungry?"

Martin was always hungry. "How about Manny's? I've been dreaming about a juicy corned beef on rye. What about you?"

"I thought you would say we should eat at Hello Deli."

"No, this is your time. I know I'll get to eat everything and anything your grandfather prepares, especially his holiday menu."

"Nothing is better," Adam said. "The turkey, sweet potatoes, salad, vegetables, dessert...all the comfort foods. After all, Thanksgiving is the one holiday that everyone celebrates."

"Except you sometimes."

"I know, but we're here now. I plan on making this a great trip and apologizing to my grandfather that I wasn't there for him as much as I should have been. I promised myself that I'm not going to be the grandson who cries over his grandfather's grave and apologizes; I am going to be the grandson he deserves. After all, he was my role model when I was growing up, not my deadbeat father."

"I've happy to hear this. I think your grandfather would like to hear you acknowledge that."

"That's because I'm the new Adam who won't disappoint him. Just because I live in New York doesn't mean I have to forget who I am. I'm his legacy."

"Are you going to tell him about Gabriella?"

"I know I said I would, but now that I'm here, maybe it's best that I just let it go. We aren't getting married, so it won't matter that much."

"It's always good to come clean," Martin said. "A moment of truth never hurts."

"You know it's always challenging to be someone you're not. I've been playing that role since college. I'm tired of all the crap I go through during the day. Sometimes, I almost believe my own bullshit."

"Wow. Did you lose consciousness on the plane or something? What prompted this turnaround?"

"It was my dream. It was so real. I feel like something's changed and it's time to rearrange my life."

"Wow, this is a whole new side of you. Where is my best friend? You know Adam, the handsome, wealthy socialite with an axe to grind?"

Adam laughed. "I'm here, but maybe I'm getting tired of just thinking about money. It's always been number one. Maybe it has something to do with my father losing so much money gambling and leaving us with nothing. After my mom died, I'm not sure where I would be if it weren't for my grandfather and grandmother."

Martin was surprised at Adam's sudden willingness to talk about his parents. "Hey, why don't you ever talk about this sort of thing? I'm always happy to listen."

"What difference would it have made? I always wanted to have more than I could ever need. Maybe you've been right all along that I stand in my own way."

"You've got that right. Honestly, though, you're making progress. Must be the Chicago air."

"Could be." Adam's smile was sincere.

* * *

They made it to Manny's in time for a quick lunch, and it was terrific. They both had salami omelets and fries. Adam had a root beer and Martin had a chocolate phosphate, his favorite. As they ate, they both had the same thought about how they missed their Saturday ritual.

"Where to next?" Adam asked. "Your choice."

"Don't take this the wrong way—"

"Okay, now I'm curious. Where do you want to go?"

"The cemetery. I want to talk to Rachel, just for a moment."

"Of course. I'm so sorry I didn't think of that. I should stop being so selfish. I'm going to work on that."

"No man, it's not you. I just don't like to know the only place I can see her is in the ground. Sorry to be so brutally honest."

Adam patted him on the back. "You know you're the strongest person I know. Without you, I probably would have married for all the wrong reasons. I want what you had. So yes, let's go see Rachel."

Adam saw a call from his grandfather but wasn't sure whether to answer. He didn't want to lie, but he also didn't want to ignore the call. This was the start of a new and more transparent life. He decided to answer.

"Hey, what's up?"

"Nothing's up with me," Zach said. "Just wondering when you're coming in." Zach waited for an answer; he could always tell when Adam wasn't telling the truth. Adam didn't necessary lie, but ever since he was a kid he tended to hold things back.

"You know we landed, don't you?"

"I do. Sorry I ruined your surprise, but your luggage arrived. Kind of a dead giveaway."

"Wow, who knew? We were going to go clothes shopping so we would have something to wear. But guess we don't need to worry about that."

"Sounds like I'll see you soon."

"Yes, but Martin wants to go the cemetery first."

"Okay. I'm at the deli, so I'll wait for you guys. You must be starving. The dinner crowd will be in soon."

"Great, sounds like a plan. See you soon."

Martin walked over.

"Guess where our luggage is?" Adam asked.

"Probably still at O'Hare. It might not even get here before Thanksgiving."

"What delivery address did you give for it to be dropped off?"

"The deli—" Martin noticed Adam's smile. "Wait, did the luggage get there?"

"It sure did. We're all good. I know we just ate, but I hope you're still hungry. He's ready for us."

"I will be," Martin said as he took a deep breath. "I'll make room."

* * *

"Okay, change of plan," Adam called out to the driver. "After the cemetery we're going to Hello Deli. Do you know how to get there?"

"Doesn't everyone?" the driver replied. "I love it there."

"Good, then you should join us," Martin said.

The driver smiled. "You don't have to ask me again. Their matzo ball soup is spectacular. I take my grandmother there whenever she's looking for soup like she used to make."

Adam smiled at Martin. "There you go, another happy camper."

"See, your grandfather still has what it takes," Martin said. "When we get to his age, I hope we're half as competent and eager to keep up such a fast pace."

"I've got news for you. Some days, I can barely get through my day. I'm not sure I have my grandfather's genes. He's unbelievable."

Martin laughed. "Well, you've got that right. I have zip but not as much as he does."

"Maybe you do. Sometimes, especially on the weekends, I get tired just watching you."

The driver tried not to eavesdrop, but he heard every word they said. He thought about how great it would be to have a friendship like theirs.

When they pulled up to the cemetery, Martin didn't get out at first. He just sat there frozen. Adam got out of the car, and the driver followed.

"Hey, mind if I ask you a question?" the driver asked.

"Go ahead. But first, I should introduce myself. I'm Adam." Adam held out his hand. "And my best friend is Martin."

"Les, Les Goldman. I was wondering how long it's been for Martin."

"How long what's been?"

"My wife died in a car crash a few years ago," Les said. "I'm trying to move on but it's hard. Very hard. My wife is buried here too. Seeing Martin sitting in the car getting up the courage to walk to her grave, I could feel his pain."

"It's been a while, but this is the first time he's wanted to come to her grave," Adam said. "I think it's a good sign. She was wonderful, the type who was everyone's friend. She was so young when she got sick, it made all of us realize how quickly life can pass us by. If we blink, we miss it all."

Les nodded. "I still have a hard time believing my wife is gone. Every morning when I look over to the other side of the bed and see she's not there, I feel the same pain I felt the day she died."

"I was never able to find the right words to help Martin. I was best man at their wedding, and I loved Rachel. I wished I could have been more help at the time. I got my second chance when Martin came to New York to help organize my life."

"You're both lucky to have each other. That matters."

"He's been my savior; he's helped me in ways no one else could. I'm lucky. But I can't take away his pain. There are days when I know he's hurting but he pretends everything is fine. My grandfather has always been there for him, and I appreciate that so much. We are better than brothers. We picked each other."

"Do you mind if I talk to him?" Les asked.

"That would be great. I'll just hang here. This is an important time for Martin. Take all the time you need."

As he watched Les walk over to the car where Martin was still sitting, Adam focused on the cool breeze and the silence. The cemetery always felt eerie to him, which was one of the reasons he never went. He loved his mother and grandmother, but he rarely visited their graves.

While he waited, he walked around the cemetery, careful not to step on any of the burial plots. Sometimes he stopped to look at a grave and wonder what that person gave to the world. He always believed everyone gives something, whether they know it or not. At least that was what his grandfather always said.

It was a while before both Les and Martin left the car. It seemed fair to say that whatever Les said helped, because Martin walked to Rachel's grave and stood there, talking to her. When Martin smiled, Adam seemed relieved. The peaceful look on Martin's face alone was worth the entire trip to Chicago.

Chapter Seven

While Zach waited for his grandson's arrival, he took center stage at the deli, pulling out a chair and standing on it. A few staffers ran over to make sure he wouldn't fall.

"Hello everyone. I have good news. My grandson Adam is on his way. When he comes in, let's give him a real Chicago welcome."

Molly was amazed how everyone listened when Zach talked. She also got a kick out of his excitement; it was contagious. It was fun to see how happy Zach was.

Charlotte walked over to Molly. "This is what family does. I love watching it."

"Charlotte, what's so special about Adam? He's just a guy."

"A gorgeous guy, and what a catch."

"Really?"

"Really. He's one of the good ones. He has literally paid back rent for some of the staff. He's paid their doctor bills when insurance didn't cover it. One time, there was a fund set up for one of the employees when his daughter had cancer. Zach mentioned it to Adam and Adam sent money to cover their bills while their daughter was getting treatment. You'll see for yourself as soon as Adam comes in how much everyone loves him."

Molly was surprised how excited she was to meet someone she had only heard about. She thought she was beyond that.

Charlotte whistled loudly and let out a deafening scream, "Yay, Adam's coming!" People across the street could have heard her. Molly laughed. Charlotte was a lively woman with a big personality, and Molly had already grown to like her. On a good day, Charlotte made everyone smile, especially when she sang along with the background music.

* * *

Zach started walking around the deli, saying hello to all the customers. He was especially happy because Adam would be arriving soon.

Charlotte was also busy talking to some of the regulars. Molly could see how much she loved the job. She also cracked jokes, knew customers' families and their problems, and knew who to treat with kid gloves. She'd already told Molly her life story, how she'd had four marriages and two dogs, but no children. Between a handsome insurance policy from a husband who died and alimony from the others, she had enough money but continued to work because she liked the deli staff and customers so much.

Zach loved Charlotte as if she were his daughter, and he knew he could count on her to help Molly adjust. He even told her about Gracie talking to him, and she wasn't judgmental at all. She loved dogs. She hadn't had any experience with one who talked, but they immediately bonded when they met. Once she knew about Gracie, Charlotte became Zach's accomplice. He knew he could trust her; she had been working for him for so many years that he lost count.

Even though he knew how strange all of this was, Zach continued to go with the flow and see what was going to happen. He was sure that if Dora was still alive, she would have called him crazy; then again, if she was alive, maybe he wouldn't be so desperate for Adam to move back to Chicago.

When Dora died, Zach lost the love of his life. For all the years they were married, she managed the household and helped him with the business. She invested their money wisely, and he didn't know how big the profits were until she passed away. It was more than Zach could ever spend, and he wished they'd been able to take advantage of it while she was around to enjoy it. Dora had always wanted Adam to find someone special, and that was a big reason why Zach made his grandson's happiness his goal.

Now here he was, hoping the plan of a mysterious little dog and the steady hands of his work family would help him make that goal a reality. There was a certain comfort in watching the pieces fall into place, as if fate had a hand in arranging all the players exactly where he needed them. Adam would arrive soon, and what could be better than that?

Chapter Eight

Zach paced near the entrance, constantly glancing at his watch and wondering when Adam would come into view. He couldn't wait to hug him and tell him how much he missed him and loved him. They talked on the phone, but in person was way better.

When the door opened and Zach saw his grandson with a smile on his face, his world became brighter. And when he hugged him, his heart was filled with joy. As for Adam, he felt like he was home. At that moment, he knew what he had been missing.

Zach hugged Martin and whispered "thank you" in his ear, then smiled at another familiar face.

"Les Goldman? As I live and breathe, I haven't seen you in forever. How's your bubbie?"

"She's good, thanks," Les said. "She's in Florida with her friends. They rented a condo for the season."

"Bring her in when she gets back."

"Will do." Les was impressed that Zach remembered him.

"How do you know the boys?"

Adam laughed. "It's a long story. Tell you later."

Meanwhile, several of the women in the deli turned their eyes toward Les. He was taller than Adam, Zach, and everyone else in the restaurant. He was more than six feet tall, with broad shoulders and a muscular build. His dark, wavy hair spilled just below his collar, but what really got everyone's attention were his sparkling blue eyes.

"Holy cow, who's the new guy in town?" Charlotte asked Molly, standing next to her. "He's mine. I'm calling him my customer wherever he sits. Hope no one minds."

"What if he's married?" Molly asked. "Either way, he's yours. I don't like married men."

Then Molly turned her attention to Adam. She was shocked by her reaction to seeing him for the first time. Her knees went weak and her heart raced. Zach had shown her some pictures of him, but she had no idea how good he looked. Not only was he cute, but there was something about his presence.

His posture was that of a successful man, perhaps even a movie star. Of course, Molly had seen other handsome men, but Adam was different. Someone should have scooped him up years ago. She had thought nothing Adam could say or do would attract her, but she was wrong. Something about him shook her to the core.

She took a few deep breaths and stepped back to get a better view. When Adam looked her way and smiled, she felt like she was sixteen again.

Charlotte laughed. "Pretty cute, isn't he?"

"I hadn't noticed." Molly tried to seem casual, but her cheeks were rosy. She couldn't hide that.

"Look at you. Wait until you get to know him. He's very charming."

"I'll bet," Molly said, watching the heartfelt reunion of Zach and Adam. Molly liked seeing how happy the two of them were to see each other. Adam shifted to shaking hands and giving kisses to some of the staff and regular customers. Molly felt like she was watching a movie.

Gracie was there too, peaking out where no one could see her. Things were going well, but she had a sinking feeling that if she didn't stay on top of everything her plan might need an update. She was always optimistic...until she wasn't.

Molly was unable to think of anything other than Adam hugging her. She began to wonder if what she felt was real.

"So, what do you think?" Charlotte asked.

"About what?"

"Never mind. I can see for myself. You're charmed like all of us."

"What do you mean?"

"Look around. Almost all the women here noticed that a very handsome man just entered the deli. Not that we don't have some good-looking customers normally, but these guys are lookers."

"You're right," Molly laughed as she looked around. She whispered to Charlotte, "Is that woman from yesterday here?"

"What woman?"

"You know who I mean. Gabriella."

"I doubt she's coming back."

"But she said she was his fiancée."

"Adam wouldn't have a fiancée without telling his grandfather."

"Got it." Molly decided not to ask any more questions; she didn't want to be nosy. It wasn't her business to collect all of Adam's history.

* * *

Zach shuffled Martin and Adam along. The hellos and hugs didn't stop; many of the customers remembered Adam from when he was just a little kid wearing a baseball cap.

Gracie maneuvered her way into all the excitement. She wanted to see Adam but didn't want to be sandwiched in. She wondered if he would recognize her.

Still all smiles, Adam stopped to introduce himself to what he thought was just a dog. "Hey, who do you belong to?"

"Me," Zach replied with pride.

"Are you kidding? You bought a dog? I asked you for years to get one, but your answer was always the same: no, no, and no." He smiled, wanting to make clear that he wasn't angry, just surprised.

"Well, life changes," Zach said. "A friend gave her to me. It's a much longer story, but we can discuss it later."

"What's her name?"

"Her name's Gracie. I didn't pick it; that was her name when I got her. Gracie and I get along just fine. She's the friend I never knew I needed."

"I'm glad. It's about time you had someone to keep you company."

Gracie gave Zach a stare that told him not to say too much yet.

Zach hugged Adam again. "We can talk about this later. Plenty of time for chitchat. Hell, you're in Chicago for

Thanksgiving. That's something I wasn't sure would happen again."

He smiled at Martin, feeling so grateful that both his boys were there to share the holiday.

Zach had a strange feeling there was more excitement to come. And then, almost on queue, his friend Nora waved to him from a table. She was sitting with a few of her friends.

Adam noticed his grandfather's reaction. "Is there something I should know?"

"No nothing, just a friend." Zach laughed and shook his head in Martin's direction.

When Zach reached over to Gracie, she whispered in his ear, "You should have told him."

The only one who overheard that was Charlotte. She laughed and started heading back to her tables. "Hate to leave this love fest, but I've got to go. I see the people at table ten looking for me."

"I think tables twelve and thirteen are also looking for you," Zach replied.

"Got to give them what they came for. They're probably looking for a better server."

Zach couldn't help but laugh. "They love you. Just give them a few desserts on the house."

"*That's* why they love me. They get free stuff. Who doesn't like free stuff?"

"Syd Bloom comes in every morning at eight and all he wants is good service. He always asks for you. If you're not here, he leaves."

"He does not!" Charlotte was adamant. "You never told me that before."

"Well, I'm telling you now. Go ahead and give table ten some goodies. And give the cheesecake special to tables twelve and thirteen. I don't know them, but I want them back."

"Already on the agenda, boss."

"Looks like nothing much has changed here," Adam said. "That's why I love this place. No matter how long I'm gone, nothing changes."

Of course, that wasn't true. A lot had changed, but Adam was so busy living his life he had no idea his grandfather had one of his own. He sometimes wondered what his grandfather did in his free time, but assumed Zach did nothing but work. He figured that ran in the family.

After a few minutes of getting caught up, Adam noticed the woman Zach had called a friend watching everything. Adam had never seen her before, but that didn't necessarily mean anything. After all, it had been several years since he came to Chicago for a visit.

Nora looked to be around Zach's age. She had blonde hair and was dressed a lot like how his grandmother used to dress. She had a furry, black coat and a matching hat, and she wore a diamond pin on her gray silk scarf. She was very stylish.

Adam noticed Nora smiling at Martin like she knew him—and the look on Zach's face convinced him there was definitely something going on. Martin had always been good at keeping secrets.

"Does everyone besides me know that woman with the hat in the first booth?" Adam asked.

"This is a long time coming," Zach said. "Her name is Nora Epstein. She lives down the block from me, but we didn't meet for years. She lost her husband years ago. When your grandmother died, she brought me casserole after casserole and left them by the door. I didn't know who was doing that at first, but one day I was driving up to the house and there she was. I invited her in and explained I didn't like casseroles, and we've been seeing each other since. She's lovely."

Adam was surprised. "How long has this been going on?"

"Three years."

"And I never knew?"

"The subject never came up. Just like Gabriella. I guess we're even."

"I think so," Martin chimed in. "Thank goodness. Keeping your secrets is tiring."

Adam just shook his head. "I guess I deserved that. How did you know?"

"She was here," Zach said. "She came by the deli and told everyone she was your fiancée, but she left before I could talk to her."

Gracie was thankful for the easy way out; that was one fewer piece of information to contend to.

Zach grabbed his grandson's hand. "Come, it's time you and Nora met."

As Zach told him more about Nora, Adam realized he was missing so much. Not only had he missed the holidays for many years in a row, but he knew he should have come for a weekend visit or two. He felt bad about not telling his grandfather about Gabriella, but he supposed there wasn't enough there to make it worth telling him. That alone was quite sad to think about. For all the mistakes he'd made in his relationships, he still had two people he couldn't live without: Martin and his grandfather.

That was when Adam noticed Molly. Reality hit him immediately: Everything was about to change. She might be the one.

Gracie was watching her plan kick into action. She whispered, "Let the magic begin."

Martin had already grabbed a table. He couldn't wait any longer, so he was noshing on his favorite chopped liver and matzo ball soup.

Zach took a seat across from him. "Are you enjoying yourself?"

"Damn straight," Martin said between bites. "I love it here."

Les was sitting back, enjoying the feeling of family. The atmosphere made him sorry he wasn't going to spend the holiday with his grandmother.

Zach patted him on the back. "Anyone new in your life?"

"Yes sir!" Les said. "Your grandson and Martin. They're two great guys."

"You've got that right. Why don't you join us for Thanksgiving? Unless you have somewhere else to be."

Les hesitated and Zach answered for him.

"Great, I'll take that as a yes." Zach never wanted to see anyone without a place to go on a holiday. "Wonderful. Then you'll come for Thanksgiving dinner."

Adam came over to the table and patted his grandfather's back. "I'm happy you have someone to be with."

"We enjoy each other's company."

"Good for you," Adam said. "Looks like you have a lot of new faces around here."

As he talked, Adam couldn't stop staring at Molly. He felt strange every time he glanced over toward her.

Zach noticed and decided to do something about it. He waved her over. "Come take a break. Molly, come sit with us."

Martin smiled, realizing Zach had some sort of plan up his sleeve.

"This is Molly," Zach said. "She's helping us here while Madeline is out. She's been in the restaurant business for years. Too bad she can't be here permanently, but we'll take what we can get."

Gracie was watching all of this, happy to see that Zach could also come up with a story under pressure.

After making sure no one could see, Gracie whispered in Zach's ear, "Way to go, Zach. I wish I would have thought of that."

Martin could sense something was going on. He pretended not to notice that Adam hadn't taken his eyes off Molly, and Zach hadn't taken his eyes off his grandson. He knew something was happening but decided not to say anything for now.

Molly could tell Adam was staring at her, and she was a little nervous about it. She didn't like the feeling of her heart beating fast, so she took some deep, cleansing breaths; her tai chi training was coming in handy.

She had promised herself Adam would be just another guy, run of the mill, someone she didn't care about one way or the other. Zach had talked him up, but she assumed those were just the opinions of a proud grandfather; she had no idea how she would feel when she saw Adam.

As it turned out, she could hardly wait to get to know him. In the back of her mind, she still wondered if he was really engaged to Gabriella. That was a definite problem. No one seemed to know anything about her, including Zach, and why wouldn't Adam tell his grandfather about her if it was true?

Chapter Nine

While chatting with his grandfather, Adam began to feel bad that he hadn't told him about his engagement. He couldn't help but rehash his last conversation with Gabriella. They always had communication problems, but he had let that go on for too long. He was engaged to a woman who meant nothing to him. His track record before her hadn't been good either, but getting engaged to her was one of his biggest regrets.

Maybe he was childish, he thought, but he didn't want his fiancée to care more about her soap operas than about him. Then again, he didn't care about her as much as he did his job. With some distance, he realized all the ways in which they weren't a team. They weren't anything, really; they were barely friends. His mind was clear that there was now no room for her in his future, and there probably never was. She would just be a memory, like most of his previous girlfriends.

Now that he was away from the hustle and bustle of New York glamor, he didn't feel like he was going to miss anything by leaving. He was standing in his grandfather's deli and, this time around, he felt like he belonged there. Being born in Chicago made him proud. He wasn't sure what had changed, but he felt a sense of calm he hadn't experienced in a long while.

Gracie was watching him, wondering if she could really get the job done. She had been watching Adam for a very long time, and his life generally progressed smoothly, though sometimes Gracie's head spun wanting him to stop and get off his dating merry-go-round.

Adam stared back at Gracie because she looked exactly like the dog in his dream. He thought the similarities with this dog his grandfather had taken in as a favor were quite a coincidence. He wasn't about to mention it to anyone because it could sound insane. Instead, he kept his thoughts to himself—his usual way of handling things.

* * *

Adam was thinking back to the night of his engagement. He knew he should have walked away and never asked

Gabriella to marry him, but it was too late for that. Now his memory of that night was haunting him.

He had spent about an hour in front of the mirror preparing what he would say. He knew Gabriella's parents weren't exactly thrilled with the idea of him as their son-in-law; he wasn't rich enough. So he never talked to them about his plans. His grandmother had always told him not to show his cards at once, so he didn't.

"Hey, Gab," he'd asked when they were back at her apartment. "Can we talk for a minute?"

"Can it wait? I need to finish my soap." That was when he should have left and never looked back. Of course, he should have left before he even asked her to marry him.

"It's important."

She laughed, making matters worse. "Adam, stop being such a bore. Come sit down. We can talk in a bit."

That was not the answer Adam was expecting. He had planned a great night out to celebrate—dinner at her favorite restaurant, a romantic walk around the park, and a movie. New York was beautiful that time of year.

"You can watch it later," he said. "I will even watch it with you. Let's go. I have a reservation. It took me weeks to get it."

"You want me to record the show? No way. It's a crucial part of the story."

Adam sat down, shaking his head, unable to imagine caring so much about strangers and their lives.

Gabriella shouted out, "Meredith, don't do it! There's another woman! Oops, too late. What a fool."

Adam knew he was the real fool. He left her apartment quietly. The next time they talked, that also didn't go well; he hadn't noticed her new hairstyle. He apologized, but if he didn't realize how one-dimensional she was before, he did then.

Now he was far away from her—and very happy about it. He couldn't imagine why she came to Chicago. And if she was there, why hadn't she called? Maybe seeing the deli was enough for her. A debutante couldn't possibly marry someone like him. To Gabriella, everything was always about money. Adam doubted she had ever heard the word "no" when she was child. He was sure he couldn't come close to giving her everything she wanted, and he didn't love her enough to try anymore.

Adam dreaded telling her that their marriage plans were off. But he made the decision and promised himself he would follow through just as soon as he was back in New York.

* * *

When Molly joined them at the table, Adam finally introduced himself. This was the moment he was waiting for since he walked into the deli. Their eyes connected immediately.

"Hello, I don't think we've met."

"No, we haven't. I'm Molly." She smiled, trying not to stare into his beautiful, dark eyes. He was gorgeous, but she reminded herself that Gabriella was also beautiful. They were a great-looking couple. She couldn't help picturing the two of them on some exotic island sitting on the beach, holding hands, and kissing nonchalantly. She felt butterflies in her stomach. She was usually very calm when dealing with men, but with Adam it seemed like time had stopped.

Zach smiled. "Well, I'm glad you kids have met."

Based on the smile on Adam's face, Zach knew he had made a great pick. It had been a long time since he saw his grandson so relaxed and happy.

What Zach saw now was the old Adam, the one he knew and loved, the caring Adam who knew right from wrong. He hoped that version of Adam would stick around. All he needed was a little push.

✳ ✳ ✳

As for Gracie, she felt like someone above was watching her. She assumed it was some sort of test to see if she could accomplish her mission. She worked well under pressure, but there was a limit. Still, the first key step was completed; Adam and Molly had met.

Gracie also had a second issue to manage, in case things weren't complicated enough. Her other assignment, which she hadn't told Zach about, was to make sure Charlotte found real love. Gracie had decided Charlotte and Martin could be a match, because now Martin seemed open to falling in love again. Gracie decided to try.

She could see Charlotte was more than happy to admire Martin. He was a little younger than her previous husbands—well, a lot younger—but she looked willing to give him a shot.

Gracie knew that Charlotte always had a way with men; after all, several had taken her to the altar. But her one wish, which remained unchanged for years, was she wanted to fall madly in love. She wanted the kind of love she saw in old movies, the romance and the sweetness. If Gracie had anything to say about it, Charlotte was going to get her wish.

Martin walked over to Charlotte as if he were reading her mind. He had known her for years and they were complete opposites, but something seemed very different now.

Neither of them saw this coming, but Gracie was overseeing it all. She was able to work magic when no one was looking.

Martin kissed Charlotte's cheek. "You're looking as beautiful as ever."

"Oh, and they say flattery doesn't work."

"Does it work for you?"

"Absolutely. I like a good compliment, a flower bouquet, and a box of chocolates. That's the least a man can do."

"Good to know." He smiled and gave her a big hug.

Charlotte was delighted to hear a compliment, especially while dressed in her server outfit. It wasn't awful, but it also wasn't particularly cute: a black T-shirt with an embroidered rose on her chest. She hadn't thought of Martin as a possibility before, but she also started to think things had changed.

She gave Martin another big hug before she returned to her tables. "Well honey, got to go. I see one of my tables turning. New ones coming in."

"I love watching a genius at work." He grinned like a child. Something between them clicked like magic.

A few relationships were blooming, and Gracie was the rare angel who could handle more than one at a time. She smiled inside. Things were going according to plan.

Chapter Ten

Other than the traditional Jewish High Holy Days, Thanksgiving was Zach's favorite holiday. He enjoyed all the food he served at his deli, but nothing compared to a great Thanksgiving turkey, his favorite challah stuffing, chestnuts, carrots, celery, and his special blend of herbs.

It was Zach's recipe, one that he had formulated himself, and no one knew the ingredients except Martin. He trusted Martin would keep his tradition going, and always wished Martin could find happiness again. He had no idea that process had already begun.

Zach was feeling like he might have his own second chance at love. Before he met Nora, he didn't think he would ever fall in love again. But the joy he felt when they were together made him feel anything was possible. Seventy was the new fifty.

He hadn't yet told Nora he felt that way and he wasn't sure what she thought about their relationship. For the time being, caring about each other was enough.

* * *

Zach's Thanksgiving dinner was just getting started. As the guests came dribbling in, Zach greeted them all. He offered them drinks and showed them to the appetizers in the living room. Zach was a great host, and anyone who walked through the doors of his home received the same attention and caring he gave them at the deli.

His guests were a mix of family, friends, and customers. Some had nowhere else to go for the holiday, but most of the guests had been coming for years and enjoyed Zach's wonderful traditions. Very few people refused an invitation from Zach.

It was a big Thanksgiving dinner because Zach had never forgotten what it was like to be on his own and start a life. His parents had brought him to Chicago from Russia, but they died when he was a teenager, and a wonderful family raised him. They were gone now, but he had promised them that he would always help others. He was never going to stop until his last breath.

Of course, one thing was very different this year. He had high hopes for Molly. He hoped Adam wouldn't get mad if he found out about what Zach had done. He'd have the right; Zach was interfering, and Adam was a very independent guy.

Molly was excited to be invited. She was looking forward to a wonderful Thanksgiving that she could always remember, just in case she never had the opportunity to be part of a family again.

Molly was happy that Phillip planned a business trip around the holiday, so she didn't have to lie and pretend she didn't want to go to Zach's for the holiday. It would be difficult to explain why she wanted to spend Thanksgiving with a family she barely knew. Part of her wondered that too.

But everything had changed for Molly the minute she walked into the deli. Zach made her feel like she belonged, and she liked it. She now knew many of the guests coming, and she was excited to experience what everyone had told her: She hadn't lived until she had been to Zach's Thanksgiving. Everyone at the deli had been talking about it. It was exciting.

She was also anxious to see what Adam was like outside the restaurant. She'd only had a few moments of conversation with Adam, and it was casual, but she wanted more.

* * *

Adam was smoking a cigarette outside his grandfather's house, deep in thought. He had no idea why Gabriella had come to the deli or where she went afterward. He hadn't been able to reach her, and he had no idea what she could have wanted. When she was mad, she usually made sure to let him know. This was strange.

Adam was prepared for her if she came back. He would break the engagement and tell her the truth. Whether he would go back into the vault of unhappy memories or not depended on the situation. His mind was a tangle of old regrets and new possibilities, and the uncertainty unsettled him more than he cared to admit.

He flicked the cigarette away, watching the thin spiral of smoke disappear into the crisp air, and glanced up just in time to see Molly stepping from the taxi. For a moment, the world seemed to slow. There was a vulnerability in the way she hesitated, glancing at the house and then smoothing her dress as if gathering courage. She looked breathtaking. Adam felt his heart jolt—a sensation both unfamiliar and electric.

Gracie was watching him through the window. It appeared Adam was enjoying the company.

Molly paused by the gate, breathing in the scent of autumn and woodsmoke, letting the anticipation steady her nerves. It was chilly, but not cold enough that she couldn't enjoy the fall air and the exhilarating aroma of the leaves falling on the grass. Tall trees and a white picket fence surrounded the suburban house. It was well-maintained and very welcoming, which didn't surprise her at all. Zach liked details.

She could hear the clatter of laughter drifting from inside Zach's house, the muffled harmonies of voices she'd only just begun to know. It felt strangely comforting, as if the warmth of the gathering inside was reaching out to invite her in. She caught Adam's eye and, for a second, neither of them looked away.

Adam, hands in his pockets, finally mustered a smile. He felt every ounce of the tension and hopefulness between them—a delicate thread that, with the right words, could either unravel or pull them closer together.

He barely knew her, but there was something strange about how he felt just looking at her. He felt a little nervous around Molly, which was surprising. He couldn't explain it, but it was there. He liked the way it felt. His life was about to change, and he had no idea if that night would be a turning point.

Adam took a step toward Molly as she closed the taxi door, her red dress glowing like a flame against the pale backdrop of the neighborhood. She smiled back, tentative but genuine, and it was all the encouragement Adam needed.

Gracie, ever the observer, shifted in her seat, her sharp gaze flicking between the two. She sensed the shift in the air and made a mental note; the night was going to be interesting.

Adam cleared his throat, trying to find the right tone—casual, yet sincere—knowing that the next few minutes might change everything.

* * *

Walking up the driveway toward Adam, Molly smoothed her hair again, straightened her dress, and took a few deep breaths. After all, she wouldn't have wanted anyone to know she tried on everything in her closet the night before and settled on the red dress just for luck.

She was both excited and nervous. Although she knew many people were coming, this dinner was still about Adam. She didn't want to look too eager because she knew the whole scenario was outside her comfort zone.

Maybe he would turn out to be selfish and uncaring, but she hoped he would have gotten some good training from Zach and his grandmother. She knew they raised him for many years and had undoubtedly been good role models.

Molly asked herself why this was such a big deal. He was just a guy.

Just because she was hired to do a job didn't mean she had to feel guilty. And what about Phillip? He was such a good guy, but she had no intention of marrying him. She started thinking she should have turned around and left when she walked into the deli the first time. Still, something inside her was making her go through with all of this.

No one would have expected Adam and Molly to be so attracted to each other immediately. Nobody except Gracie. She was happy the two of them had a connection, but the fact that Gabriella had come and gone was still concerning. They were still engaged, meaning things weren't falling into place the way she had hoped. Gracie always had to be on her toes, and she had a lot riding on their connection.

Still, if this were an easy match, they wouldn't have needed her help. She still imagined she could bring these two people together.

* * *

Adam continued down the driveway to meet Molly.

"Hi. Why didn't you say you needed a ride? I would have picked you up. I'm sure my grandfather would have given me the keys to his car, although he didn't like the way I drove before I went to New York."

"Did it get better there?"

"Possibly even worse." He laughed, and so did she.

As they walked up the stairs onto the porch, Adam changed the subject.

"Molly, you look fantastic. Red is your color."

"Thanks. I'm not used to someone noticing what I wear."

"I find that hard to believe."

There it was, that moment Molly had worried about. Besides being gorgeous, he was nice. Very nice. She felt attractive and maybe even a little sexy. Molly and Adam looked into each other's eyes, studying one another. Adam had a strange look on his face as if he were somewhere else. What he didn't know was he was falling in love.

Molly was starting to feel a little uncomfortable making conversation with a man who had no idea he was part of a setup.

"Should we go in now?" she asked.

"Sounds like a plan. Let's go." He held out his hand, leading the way.

"It smells great in here."

"I must admit it does. My grandfather's been cooking up a storm."

"I can imagine. He's been trying out some new recipes and, let me tell you, they are good. Very good."

"Stick with me." Adam smiled. He could have said anything, and she would have liked it. His voice was so charming she felt like she was in a movie, and he was the guy who came to sweep her away and disappears—but in a movie, he comes back.

Gracie was watching Adam like a hawk. She was hoping they would connect in a romantic, loving way, but she also knew there was a long way to go before the spark ignited. She shook her head. She could tell Molly was having doubts, and hoped Molly wasn't going to give up on love if things with Adam didn't click perfectly. Gracie was starting to wonder if she had to alter her plan and was hoping someone would help her out.

When she saw Charlotte whispering in Adam's ear, she knew the situation was handled.

"Sweetie, your grandfather is in the library," Charlotte told him. "He needs to speak to you pronto."

"Can it wait?" Adam whispered back.

When Charlotte shook her head, Adam excused himself. "Charlotte, can you keep Molly company?"

"For sure. Come on hon, let's get a drink."

When Adam was gone, she turned to Molly. "So, he's pretty cute, isn't he?"

"He's not bad."

"Hey, you might need a few drinks if you haven't noticed how gorgeous the guy is."

"I agree he's cute."

Charlotte took her by the hand and off they went to the bar. "Good thing you noticed. Otherwise, I would think you're dead."

* * *

Zach was waiting for his grandson in the den. He was holding a box and a letter.

"I don't know what's inside," he began. "But someone dropped this off for you last night."

"Why didn't you give it to me then?"

"You needed some sleep and I assumed it could wait until today."

They each took a seat, Adam on the couch and Zach in his favorite leather thinking chair. Zach was the only one who ever sat there; it wasn't a rule, but it seemed like no one else belonged there.

Zach watched as his grandson read the letter, crunched up the paper, and threw it in the garbage. Adam didn't say anything until he opened the box and smiled. Then he let out a big laugh and breathed a sigh of relief.

"I assume that means it was good news?"

"The best," Adam said. "Gabriella came to Chicago to break the engagement."

"Oh, I see. So, you didn't actually want to marry the woman you asked to marry you. Am I right?"

"You are. Let me read the letter to you."

"That's okay. It's your private business."

"When did you ever not want to know good news?'

"Are you saying I'm nosy?"

"Precisely. And she sent me the ring." Adam opened the box and there it was—gorgeous and quite big. He passed it over to his grandfather.

"Wow, you must know the right people."

"That's true. You know I make a lot of money."

"I do. Sorry. It's just this whole engagement thing. To think you would get a ring for someone I never met and were planning a wedding without me knowing anything about it made me sad."

"I think I never told you about it because I knew it was never going to happen. I never loved her."

"Is that supposed to make me feel better?"

"Yes, I hope so," Adam in a sheepish voice. "Let me read you the note."

"Okay. If you feel you want to."

Adam sat back against the couch and read aloud:

Dear Adam,

I know this is an unusual way to end a relationship, let alone an engagement. As you know, marriage is difficult enough when you love someone. But you know we don't love each other, now or ever. It seemed like a good thing to do for my parents because you were grounded and nice, even though they never liked you.

I'm sure you won't be shocked, but I've found someone else. My parents hate him, but I love him. He's not what they would have hoped for, but they were never there for me when I was growing up. I'm telling you this now because we have never had even one heart-to-heart discussion, mostly because I never wanted one. I know you tried, but it was never going to happen.

I hope you find someone who will love you the way you should be loved. You're a wonderful person. I'm sorry that I didn't love you, but it's just not in me.

Please tell Martin that I'm very sorry I treated him so badly, but I think I was always *jealous of your friendship. And he was right. I was never the right one for you but there is someone out there who will be.*

Love who you are
Gabriella

Zach stood up and reached for Adam, pulling him in for a hug. They hugged for a long time.

"I have an idea," Zach said. "Let's go out and have a good time with our friends and family. Next time, please don't shut me out. I'm here for anything you need. There's no one in the world who I love more. So please, for as many years as I have left, let's try to never let each other down. That is real love, and that will be my legacy to you."

Chapter Eleven

When Adam walked back into the crowd, he was looking for Molly.

He didn't see her at first, but she was there chatting and laughing. Once he found her, Adam couldn't take his eyes off Molly. He had felt something on their first hello that he had never felt before.

There had been so many strange coincidences lately. It scared him a bit, and he wanted to understand why. He wondered about a lot of things, starting with his repeated dreams about a dog talking to him. He felt like life was becoming a puzzle that he was supposed to figure out. He hated doing puzzles even as a child; he preferred actual facts over confusing questions. But for now, he was going to try having a good time without overthinking everything.

He tapped Molly's shoulder. "Sorry that took so long."

"Is everything okay?" She hoped Zach hadn't told him the truth about why she was there. Then again, he wasn't ignoring her; if he knew, he might have left the party. Molly had a few questions of her own, but she didn't want to appear eager to delve into his life. She proceeded with caution.

"Are you happy to be back in Chicago?" she asked. "I haven't been to New York, but I might go there some day."

"You can visit me. I'd be happy to show you around. I like it there. But now that I'm here, I realize how different it is. I might miss Chicago more than I thought."

"Different in a good way?"

"It's peaceful and I kind of like that. That's one thing about living in Manhattan. It's never quiet."

"Your grandfather told me how much you love New York. But he misses you so much."

"I miss him too."

"Zach's such a great guy. He's made me feel like I'm important. It happened immediately. He was so kind."

"Yes, he is. If my grandfather acted that way, it's because he meant it. He doesn't have a fake bone in his body. He always told me the truth is the most important thing in life."

Molly started to feel guilty about what she and Zach were hiding.

"I wish I enjoyed holidays more," Adam admitted.

"From what I've heard, Thanksgiving is his very favorite one."

"You haven't seen anything yet. This is his holiday and almost everyone here knows that. Though, when I was a kid, he also really loved Halloween."

Molly smiled. "I bet he did. He seems to love fun, and Halloween is exciting and fun."

"His house was the one where all the kids congregated. To tell you the truth, his baked pumpkin seeds were great. My friends used to come over to have some and watch him bake them. He really enjoyed doing that for all of us. My grandmother didn't like Halloween, but she always enjoyed watching him carve the pumpkins. He had so much fun doing it. Even when I came home from college, I still loved watching him."

Molly was shocked at how open Adam was being about his childhood. It was nice hearing more about Zach, of course, but mostly she liked listening to Adam share his stories with her.

"If this is too much, let me know," he said. "I could go on and on about him."

"Keep going. I love hearing about him. I wish I had a grandfather to talk about."

Adam smiled at her. "I have no idea why I'm telling you all of this. I don't usually talk about my life. It just seems to be coming out."

Gracie was just out of sight, jumping up and down that somehow Molly and Adam had found so much common ground. They had found a space that was comfortable for both of them, not realizing destiny was bringing them together.

But right at the moment it looked like a bond was forming, Gracie felt her heart rate going up. She had been so engrossed in their conversation that she almost missed an important element.

"Thanksgiving is so important to my grandfather that he always picks out everything that is going to be on the menu, even though he hires the best caterers," Adam continued. "He's always concerned that he might not be able to spend enough time with his guests and still be in the kitchen and make the holiday the very best."

Molly wasn't sure where Adam was going with the conversation, but she liked hearing about what a wonderful person Zach was.

"Funny thing is my grandfather could have been a successful caterer. He would have been on everyone's list for parties or any other function where people need caterers. He would be in *Who's Who*."

"But he's a successful restaurateur." Molly reminded herself about the conversation she had with Phillip after she said yes to the job at the deli. She couldn't let Adam say that about his grandfather; she thought it was disrespectful.

Adam sensed something changed. "I don't mean he isn't successful. He's one of the best restauranters in Chicagoland. I just thought he could have doubled or even tripled his income."

"Maybe he's not motivated to think about money all the time. Are you ashamed of him?"

"No, of course not. It's just that he's quite different than me."

"Meaning you're better than him?"

"Of course not. He's such a good man. And I love him so much for always caring for me, even when I didn't make it easy. He always gave me the benefit of the doubt. Without his help, I would be nothing. He gave me the tools to help me survive. I came here to try making up for all the years I didn't come home for the holidays."

Gracie inched closer so she could hear what they were saying. She thought this was the make-or-break moment.

"From what I can see, your grandfather loves you no matter what," Molly said. "He needs to hear you say that to him. Everyone, including Zach, needs to hear how greats he is."

Adam was a little shocked. She seemed to know his grandfather so well. Was there something he didn't know?

"So sorry," Molly said. "It isn't my place to say anything."

Gracie was breathing harder, sending up an SOS. For a moment, everything seemed in slow motion. Just as Gracie was taking a moment to regroup, Charlotte came over to save the day.

"Well look at you two," Charlotte said. "Cutest couple ever. I didn't see it at first—but now, yes sir. I love a good match."

Adam and Molly both suddenly seemed a little shy, not sure what to make of the moment.

"Are you matchmaking?" Molly asked.

"Maybe a little."

Adam had a second to make things right. He worried he'd given Molly the wrong idea. He would never be ashamed of his grandfather.

"Back to my point," Adam pivoted from what Charlotte had said. "Molly, I'm so sorry you thought I meant something different. I want you to know I think you got the wrong impression of me."

"Did I?"

"I was just blabbing, not thinking about how it came out. I would never, ever insult the man I owe everything to. He made me a better man because he's the man who has everything. There were times when I was down and, if it wasn't for him, I wouldn't be the man I am today. Can we shake on this and forget the conversation so far? I need a second chance."

Molly was impressed by his honesty. And his smile was as intimate as a kiss. She couldn't resist his charm.

"Deal."

Neither of them noticed when Charlotte walked away; they continued talking as if nothing happened. But something did. An undeniable magnetism was building between them.

* * *

Gracie was starting to think this might be easier than she imagined, but she was superstitious enough not to count on anything yet.

Molly and Adam were right there, hanging on by a thread. Gracie wanted to hear everything they said, and she wanted to do it in person. By this point, everything was crucial. No room for mistakes, or it would be a long time before Gracie got another assignment.

"I've never celebrated a holiday like this with so many people," Molly said, enjoying the rich aroma of turkey and freshly baked bread. She felt the same way when she first walked into the deli. She was going to have a family dinner with people she had started to care about, including Adam.

As they walked closer to the dining area, they were greeted by laughter and lots of side chatter. Molly was amazed at how nice everyone from the restaurant looked; everyone cleaned up pretty nicely.

Adam looked around and saw all the familiar faces from his past, plus several new ones. "Tonight," he said to Molly, "you will see and hear things like you've never seen before. This is quite a mix of personalities."

As he said that, he noticed Gracie was beside him. He couldn't help wondering why his grandfather got a dog at this point in his life—and why she looked so much like the dog in his dreams. Usually, he would laugh at something like that and brush it out of his mind, but it felt too strange. So did the story his grandfather told him about his friend Joe giving him Gracie as a gift. Everything that happened since he got to Chicago seemed too coincidental.

While he was thinking, Adam noticed Martin was standing very close to Charlotte. It wasn't like this was the first time they had seen each other. But it appeared they were having a lot of fun and Martin was laughing. For that alone, Adam was grateful. To see him having fun made him feel like Martin was coming alive.

"Molly, can I get you a drink?" Adam asked.

"Maybe a little later. I'm too busy taking all this in."

"I'll be right back. Don't want to leave you alone; I know it's a bit overwhelming. But you'll be fine."

"That's so nice of you. I'm going to be fine. It's just going to take a little more chatting and, hopefully, the butterflies in my stomach will disappear before it's dessert time."

"Happy to help. If my grandfather likes you, that's good enough for me. I have been known to be a gentleman at times."

Trying to relax, Molly took a deep breath and smiled.

"Well, in that case, I wouldn't want to disappoint you. I'll take a ginger ale with lots of ice. Oh, and a lemon slice."

"Coming up. Be back before you know I'm gone."

"Sounds wonderful." Charlotte was right; Adam was charming and so much more. Molly didn't want him to be nice, but he was, and her plan of not getting involved was going out the window.

Molly prided herself on always being cool and calm, but she was feeling nervous. She hoped no one could tell how uncertain she felt at that moment, especially Adam. And what if he found out how she came to be there? She couldn't let that happen.

Adam returned quickly, just like he said. She was glad about that; it gave her less time to think about the fact that Adam's grandfather put this whole deal together. Then again, she was the one who answered the post.

As Adam handed her the glass, the touch of his hand against her skin stopped her for a moment. She was frozen. There was a part of this that she couldn't seem to understand. The week before she was just plain Molly Parker, ordinary and trying to find herself. Now she stood there looking at someone she would never have met in her world, but she was happy that she met him.

Adam watched her, wondering what she was thinking. "You seemed to disappear for a second."

"No, I'm right here. Thank you for the drink."

There it was, another moment when she wanted to kiss him. But once she did, this would be real. If she kept her distance, it might be easier to leave. Molly didn't want to care about him at all, much less so fast.

"I'll be back in a few," she said. "I want to say hello to some of the staff."

All she wanted was to go somewhere and think. She didn't know the house well, so she decided to wing it. Molly worked her way to the kitchen. Maybe there she could do something to help. Sometimes doing something was better than letting her mind go wild.

Molly was just someone in the crowd and knew she could easily slip away. She hated to deceive Zach, but she didn't want to be in the mix anymore. Adam was engaged and she had Phillip. That was enough of a mess. She wished she had never used that dating site. She needed answers—and to be honest with herself.

That's when she noticed a pantry in the back of the kitchen. She decided she could hide out there, but she wasn't going to be alone for long. Adam followed her.

* * *

For a moment, neither of them said a word. They looked at each other like something special was about to happen. Molly wanted to kiss him, but she wasn't about to initiate a romance that was never going to happen. As far as she was concerned, she shouldn't have let this whole scheme go this far.

Gracie was there too, but neither of them could see her. She was sipping a martini to calm her nerves. She was certain a kiss would be too early, but now things were out of her control. She watched and waited.

Adam had something to say, and finally it just came out. "Despite all the reasons we shouldn't be together, I can't help myself. I fell for you like a ton of bricks."

Molly, not holding back anymore, kissed him. He gathered her in his arms and held her tightly. The touch of his lips on hers felt right. She had never been kissed like that. They both assumed this was perfection.

But Gracie wasn't sure. Something still wasn't quite right.

Adam smiled. "Now what?"

Molly thought for a moment before responding. The kiss was perfect—but the situation wasn't.

"Well, to start with, you should tell your grandfather that you're engaged."

Adam was surprised she knew. "Does everyone know about Gabriella?"

"They sure do. It's a close-knit circle your grandfather has created, so of course information travels."

"Funny you should say that. Gabriella and I are not engaged anymore. She gave me back the ring. It's over. Done. Finito. Adios."

"Really?" Molly was shocked. Suddenly, she felt like just a rebound romance. It was a great kiss, but there was so much more at stake.

Gracie knew this might be dangerous. Things were moving too fast. *This can't be good*, she thought.

"Okay, my turn," Molly said, though she knew what she had to say wouldn't help the situation. "I live with someone. We share our lives to a point, but it's complicated."

"Does he love you?"

"He does."

"And do you love him?"

"I don't know."

"I don't know what that means. Why aren't you married?"

"Because I don't love him. At least, I think I don't. He wasn't my destiny. He was my stopping place until I decide what my life is going to be." Molly stopped herself right there; she had said too much already.

Adam's heart was beating fast. He was not in control, and he didn't like that one bit. They kissed again. But it wasn't the same. Something had changed suddenly and, when they looked at each other, the spark wasn't there anymore. Neither of them said anything. A lot was going on in the kitchen and they needed privacy.

Gracie was disappointed as she watched something that was supposed to be beautiful and now wasn't. She had tears in her eyes, thinking she had failed. She needed to figure out what was missing, and she had to do it soon. She felt a cold breeze surround her and realized that something bad was going to happen. She knew what that meant. She was being tested.

Gracie watched as Adam brushed Molly's hair from her face. He touched her so sweetly. "I'm just so confused by all of this," he said. "Please forgive me if I'm going too fast. I hope I didn't scare you away."

Molly shed a few tears because everything had shifted. She didn't speak because she was sad. The wonderful kiss they had shared seemed just a fleeting moment in time.

And then it happened. The smoke alarm went off.

* * *

As Adam and Molly ran out of the pantry and into the kitchen, there was smoke everywhere. They could barely see. People were screaming and calling out for each other in fear. Just moments earlier, the kitchen was buzzing with the savory smell of spices and simmering sauces. The counters were full of pans and silver foil covering several of the pans to keep the food warm.

The fire was not just a small kitchen fire; it was a blazing inferno. A small flame had flared up while a pan was unattended and burst into flames. Nothing the chefs tried stopped the burning flames from damaging the entire array of foods and baked goods. Everything that smelled good minutes ago was now gone.

"Get water and call 9-1-1!" one of the chefs called out. Everything was happening so fast as the kitchen became chaotic and filled with thick, black smoke. All the jokes and funny stories people were telling a few minutes earlier were now forgotten.

The fire department arrived faster than anyone could have expected, but smoke was already filling the living room and everywhere else. The kitchen looked like a battlefield, and everyone was rushing to get out of the house.

Many of the guests were crying from fright and coughing from the thick smoke. Their faces were painted with ashes from the flames. Soon the house was flooded with firefighters and police officers making sure everyone was outside. While the responders were helping everyone out, Molly refused to leave without finding Zach. It was hard to breathe, but she wanted to make sure he left and didn't try to do anything heroic.

As she feared, she found him still inside, helping some of the others. She grabbed him and pulled him out of the house. "Let the firefighters do their work," she said. "You don't need to be the hero this time."

Everything happened so fast that it hadn't occurred to Molly that Gracie was somewhere in the crowd. Once Zach was outside, Molly rushed back in, realizing a dog had no choice but to run out unattended or maybe die from smoke inhalation. When she found Gracie, she picked her up and took her outside. Gracie pretended to be afraid, but she knew she was safe; she was an angel, after all. Once she knew everyone else was okay, she worried more about her plan literally going up in smoke.

Martin and Charlotte were also helping the officials, and the rest of the staff joined them. They weren't just employees; they were heroes. They made sure every last person was out of the house and safe.

* * *

There was a large crowd outside, including some of the neighbors. All the guests were rescued quickly. Everyone was accounted for, and nobody was seriously injured.

Adam stood next to his grandfather with their arms linked together. Zach was relieved everyone was safe. A house could be replaced, but people couldn't.

Molly was standing off to the side when she heard a voice. It was Phillip calling out to her. "Molly, honey, are you okay?"

She was so happy to see him she began to cry. "What are you doing here? I thought you were out of town for a meeting."

"I was, but it's Thanksgiving and I let you down. I'm so sorry. I should have spent it with you. Can you forgive me?"

Molly coughed a few times. Despite her tears, she wrapped her arms around Phillip and kissed him the same way she kissed Adam. But this time, she felt something she hadn't felt with Phillip before.

Gracie was watching. She had no idea anything like that was going to happen but, just the same, she was happy to see love happening. Maybe that was why she was there. Sometimes the higher-ups played games with angels just to see if they could handle the unexpected.

* * *

While Zach was thankful that nobody was killed or badly injured, he was still devastated by the seriousness of the situation. When he saw Gracie sitting on the edge of the driveway, he was happy to see she was also fine. He took a deep breath and looked up. "Thank you," he said softly.

With all that had happened, Zach didn't forget why they were all there: Thanksgiving. At the top of his voice, he yelled out, "Thank you to everyone. Even though tonight's dinner was ruined, there's always tomorrow. Please go home and get some rest. Tomorrow at six, we'll all have Thanksgiving at the deli."

Zach paused and looked around.

"And to all my neighbors, I appreciate you so much for bringing out blankets and coats for my guests. Please have dinner with us tomorrow. And all you firefighters and police officers are invited to join us at the deli if you can."

Adam stepped forward. "I also want to thank everyone for helping tonight," he said. "I know my life changed forever while I watched and waited for everyone to get out safely. I've decided I will be coming home to Chicago for good. I miss everyone and I want to share my life with my grandfather at the deli! He can take off a few days now and then because I'll be by his side."

"I second that!" Matin called out from the crowd. Then he surprised everyone by kissing Charlotte, lifting her up, and twirling her around.

"Are you ready to take a chance on me?" he whispered in Charlotte's ear.

She looked up and smiled. "I certainly am. This one's a keeper."

Everyone who had stayed behind was clapping with joy.

The firefighters blocked off the house with tape, ensuring that no one was allowed back in. They wanted to confirm that all sparks were extinguished and the house was free of fire. No stone would be left unturned.

Zach's eyes filled with tears as he watched everyone leave, waving to his guests. Adam called for a reservation at a nearby hotel, and he and Martin went with Zach so they could help him cook in the morning. But first, they were going to get some sleep, whether Zach liked it or not. As for Gracie, she couldn't stay at a hotel, so Molly said she and Phillip would take her home with them.

The plan was turning out differently than any of them expected. It wasn't Gracie's plan after all, but one coming from the boss above her, one meant to show everyone that even when things go wrong, there's always hope.

Chapter Twelve

What a difference a day made. After a restless night, Martin, Adam, and Zach decided to get to the deli before anyone else arrived. The entire staff had committed to coming and helping because they knew how hard it would be for Zach not to celebrate his favorite holiday.

Zach wanted to decorate the deli like he did his house. He wanted it to look cozy. But he didn't have the decorations he needed, so he sent both Adam and Martin on a treasure hunt knowing it was a difficult task the day after Thanksgiving.

But when Zach unlocked the door, the deli was already decorated with autumn leaves everywhere and paper turkey cutouts hanging around the room. It looked like the deli was being photographed for a magazine. The lighting was unique, and the smell of freshly baked bread and savory spices filled the air. Zach though he might be dreaming, but then he saw Gracie and Molly.

Molly had taken Gracie home as promised, and Zach didn't know they would be coming. After he saw her leave with Phillip, part of him wondered if he'd ever see Molly again.

Molly hugged Zach. "Did you sleep?"

"Not a wink. I'm so sorry everything got so out whack. It's my fault all of this happened. I should have never put that ad online."

Gracie shook her head. "No way, Zach. It wasn't your fault; it was just life happening before your eyes. Sometimes plans change, but I'm still here. I'm not ready to leave you just yet. And I have some good news. You thought Nora wouldn't be able to come to your Thanksgiving dinner, but she's coming today. Her plane was grounded due to bad weather, so she'll join you today and celebrate with her children next week."

"Was that your doing or an actual weather problem?" Zach asked her.

"You'll just have to accept the fact that there are some things you'll never figure out," Gracie said with a wink.

The music in the kitchen was a little louder than usual, but this party needed music. When Zach checked the back, most of the food was already in the process of being cooked. Zach's entire staff—including Madeline, who had never cooked a day in her life—was cooking. All that was left for Zach to make was the stuffing. It wouldn't be Thanksgiving if he didn't make it with his secret recipe, and he was happy to get to work.

Zach couldn't understand what really happened the night before. A lot of things were moving quickly. Adam seemed like he really wanted to come home, and Martin was surprisingly happy with Charlotte by his side. On the romance front, it looked like Molly realized she might actually want to spend the rest of her life with Phillip, with no hard feeling about their whole chaotic plan. He thought maybe it had helped her learn a few life lessons. And Gracie was staying on because there was still more work to do.

* * *

As the guests arrived, everyone was happy to see each other and glad everyone came out uninjured. Their luck was surprising to many, but not to Gracie. She had a feeling it had been part of the plan and nobody needed to get hurt.

The music was cheerful—a mix of classic holiday music with a touch of "Oh Chanukah" thrown in. Everyone was wearing festive attire, and the laughter and chatter were nonstop. Les sang a few songs to lift everyone's spirits. It worked; he had a wonderful voice. Gracie had her eye on him, thinking he might be next on her list. She had a feeling he needed someone to love, and she was on the lookout.

There were some changes to the menu, of course, but everyone seemed to be enjoying themselves so much that no one minded. There were platters of deli meats, including pastrami, salami, and roast beef. Along with fresh turkey sandwiches, there were a few basic green bean casseroles, sweet potatoes with marshmallows, and Martin's favorite chopped liver. To wrap up the party, everyone—including many of the firefighters and police from the night before—received a goody bag full of chocolates and cookies.

Everyone seemed thrilled with being together and celebrating. It was a delightful holiday meal full of love and sharing. It didn't matter where they were as long as they had delicious food, fun, and wonderful connections that made the night unforgettable. It wasn't about the beautiful china, classic crystal glasses, or expensive silverware; it was about the warmth and commitment that held them together.

It was an unforgettable Thanksgiving at the deli.

The End

About the Author

I'm Marsha Casper Cook the founder and producer of all the Michigan Avenue Media podcasts on Blog Talk Radio.

She has over 25 years of experience in the writing industry with 14 books (five of which are children's books), and 11 feature-length screenplays. Several of her screenplays have optioned by production companies.

My Podcast guests give our listeners info that you might not find anywhere else because many of them choose the topics we discuss. Because I interview people from all walks of life the shows are always exciting.

My latest accomplishment is I am now a contributor to *eYs International Magazine*. To find out more about my shows and my books visit these websites and links:

@Marshacaspercook.com | Linktree

www.michiganavenuemedia.com

http://www.marshacaspercook.com

http://www.marshaskidsbooks.com

All of Marsha's books are available in print, ebook and Audible formats on Amazon.com